forgetting him

Originally Titled Lost on the Way

isabel jolie

ISABEL JOLIE

The minute I heard my first love story, I started looking for you, not knowing how blind that was. Lovers don't finally meet somewhere. They're in each other all along.

— Rumi

one

Jason

The light cracking through the window hits me like a laser beam splitting my skull open. Pain lances through my head. My arm aches, and a thousand needles stab repeatedly. I flex my fingers. And freeze.

A mass of brown strands rest on the crook of my arm. Messy, bedridden hair hides her face. Holy. Fuck. *What have I done?*

The rumpled white sheet falls below her bare waist and continues onto mine. Her porcelain skin shimmers in the light, and her long brown hair winds down her chest. The tawny orb of her nipple peeks under the mahogany locks, and a flashback of my mouth on that very nipple has me twisting away and jumping out of bed.

I stumble into a wall, my morning wood sticking out like a welcoming flag, and cringe, looking over my shoulder to see if my sudden departure woke her. She shifts onto her stomach, and her hair tumbles downward, covering her shoulder. On a silent exhale, I pick up my boxers from the floor, and stumble to the kitchen.

There were drinks—I remember drinks. Tequila. I told her I'd never done a body shot before. She shrieked and unbuttoned her white shirt, displaying her lace bra. That naughty bra I've wondered about because you can see the edge of the lace through her white t-shirts. I've wondered if it's sheer or lightly padded. It's sheer.

I push the button on the coffee machine and close my eyes. The outline of her nipples through that bra comes to mind. My tongue licking up the salt and lime. How badly I wanted to reach up and hold those two palm-size breasts, perky and erect. How good they tasted…no, she tasted.

My hold on the counter tightens as I aim to shake those thoughts. The coffee drips slowly, filling up the glass pot. I watch each drop, teeth grinding, as anger at what I've done, what I let happen, resonates. A vision of me pounding her, her legs around me, hits me hard. My life. Fucked by tequila. I spin around as if making a one-eighty will eliminate the memory.

She's standing there, her back to the counter, watching me. I didn't hear her come in. She's wearing an old t-shirt of mine, and it falls mid-thigh. She's not wearing a bra.

Determining if Maggie's wearing a bra, and if so, what kind of bra, is the one pastime I've allowed myself over the years. Really, that's Adam's fault. There was this nurse. Unbelievably, named Nurse Florence, but she let us call her Nurse Flo. That woman could deadlift me. And she had breasts. Massive ones. That's what started Adam and his game. Not so much to do in a hospital bed.

"Hey, what size bra do you think Nurse Flo wears?" The

two of us laughed like juvenile eight-year-olds over that stupid question. We Googled it. No. Google wasn't so big back then. We Yahooed that shit. The game kind of grew from there. Pervy, but it passed the time. Now, it's a habit—a habit that somehow evolved into "guess which kind of bra Maggie is wearing today." Her breasts are on the smaller side, but if she's wearing a padded push-up, she has more contours and becomes a C cup. But I prefer the smooth, thin bras. If she's wearing a soft cotton shirt, sometimes her nipples point, and the outline can be seen through the thin fabric. The absolute best is no bra. Obviously.

Thinking back on the "what-size" day has me smirking a bit, even though my world is upside down right now. Mags smiles too, as if she's in my head, reliving that memory of me and Adam bored in our hospital gowns. But nah, that's a world she doesn't really get. Can't get. Although not for her lack of trying. May she never, ever know.

I rub my fingers through my hair, staring at her. Even hungover, she's adorable. *Fuck. Adam.*

She rotates her foot on the floor. "Coffee?" she asks, timid. I turn back around to get a mug, cursing myself. This is why I've never let this shit happen. I mix in a Stevia pack and skim milk, stir, and give it to her, while staring at the large tile squares butting up to the corner cabinets. A film of gray dust darkens the edge.

Maggie lifts the mug to her mouth, sips, then sets it down on the counter. She steps to the refrigerator and pulls out the half-gallon of fresh-squeezed juice. She's so hungover she can't drink coffee. That's telling.

She pours herself a tall glass of an orange concoction. It's a blend of carrot, lemon, apple, banana, kale, and honey. She read somewhere it boosts immunity. She keeps my fridge stocked with the stuff. Ever since we moved to New York, she's done it. Back at college in New Hampshire, we'd meet up for coffee first, then after our first class, hit the juice place. Freshly squeezed vegetables. Maggie's nirvana.

She's stayed over tons. So, of course, she knows where my clothes are and her way around the kitchen. Twelve years of friendship. I've been good. Never strayed. Made a move. When her arm lifts to tilt the glass back and empty it, the hem of the t-shirt rises, and her smooth, lean thigh catches my eye. Now I know firsthand just how silky smooth that skin is.

"Jason, please…. Jason, right there… Jase… Jase, fuck." Her words from last night punch me in the gut like a series of one-two jabs. My grip on my coffee cup tightens as the memory of sliding into her courses through me. How good, warm, tight she felt. Fuck. I stare at the popcorn ceiling. Did we use a condom? I was drunk. But not too drunk. Obviously. Fuck.

She finishes her glass and rinses it, then sets it in the dishwasher. When she turns to face me, I grimace. "Did we use a condom?" Shit. This is Mags. My best friend in the whole fucking world. Adam's girl.

Those brown-bronze eyes cast downward, a hint of pink along her cheekbones, below her smattering of freckles. Freckles. She and I share freckles in common. Her chest rises before she answers. "I don't think so."

"Should we go get a morning-after pill?"

Her gaze drops to the floor, and fuck if guilt doesn't pour through me, a weight pulling me down, drowning me. She stares at her socks when she answers. "No. I don't think so. The timing's not right." She mumbles something that sounds like something, something, "period tracker."

Then she's running down the hall, and it's as if she's running away from me. She flings the bathroom door open, and I hear her gag. Fuck. This is how hungover she is. I step into the small half bath and bend down to pull her hair back. Not the first time I've done this.

When she stands, I run warm water over a washcloth and gently swab at her mouth. She bats my hand away, and I pull her to me to hold her tight. "Hey, we're okay, right? Still friends?"

Her head brushes against my chest as she nods, and the vise on my chest loosens. I relax my hold on her to lead her back to the bathroom attached to my bedroom. I pull out her toothbrush from the small drawer below the counter where I store it, should she ever need it, run it under the water, put some toothpaste on it, and pass it to her. Then I close the bathroom door behind me because she'll want privacy.

As I pull on a pair of sweatpants and a t-shirt, the framed picture on top of my dresser seizes my attention. It's a photo of Adam, Maggie, and me. The car behind us is Adam's black Jeep, fully loaded with both Adam's and Maggie's stuff. They left that day for a summer cross-country road trip, touring the Great Lakes and doing whatever else to reach his home in California. We're all smiling. Happy. Freshman year at Dartmouth behind us. Maggie gave it to me for Christmas the following year. A couple of months after the funeral.

The bathroom door opens. Maggie slips out and gathers her clothes from the floor. Her bra lies half-draped on the lampshade, and she lifts it, her back to me. Without speaking a word, she returns to the bathroom and closes the door.

I head to the kitchen for a fresh cup of coffee. I'm pouring milk into my mug when Maggie calls from the apartment door, "I'm gonna head out. See you later, okay?"

The door closes before I can respond. I tilt my head back until it hits the wall behind me. Fuck!

On a normal hungover day, she'd stay. We'd groan, swear to never drink again, order in a greasy early lunch, then Netflix it on the couch all afternoon.

And now she's gone. My head throbs, and my stomach lurches with a queasiness I'm far too familiar with. *What the hell have I done?*

two

Maggie

I tap lightly on Yara's bedroom door then push it open when I hear, "Come in." Yara's leaning back on several stacked pillows, snuggled below comforters, the glow from her phone the only light source. With extra care, I set the brown cardboard coffee-holder down on her mattress, along with the white bag holding the breakfast I picked up during my walk of shame home, and raise the blinds in the room.

"What the hell happened to you?" Yara, my longtime roommate, asks while she lifts her coffee out of the tray.

I grab one of her pillows, drop onto her bed, and bury my face in the downy softness.

"That bad, huh?"

I whimper then sit up and pull the pillow into my lap. I grab my coffee and grimace before opening up. "It happened."

Yara sips her coffee and squints as she studies me. I

haven't actually looked in a mirror, but I'm assuming she's noticing that the bun on top of my head consists of a twisted rat's nest. She leans forward and runs a finger across my neck. "Is that a hickey?"

Fuck. I hop off the bed and stand before her dresser, shifting in the light. There's an odd-shaped reddish formation at the base of my neck, and as I twist to the side, there's another similar marking below my ear. *Damnit, Jason. I work with children.*

Yara leans back on the bed and chomps on the buttered bagel I brought back for her. While chewing, she connects the dots and shrieks, "Holy shit! It happened. You and Jason finally did the deed. It's about damn time."

I study the markings on my neck a moment longer before collapsing on the bed beside her and cover my face with my hands. If this day could just go away, that would be fantastic.

Yara lifts my arm and peers down at me. "Not so good?"

"I don't know. I just…don't know. He asked me if we used a condom. That was, like, the first thing he said to me. I don't think that's a good sign, do you? That's more of a 'wow, we really screwed the pooch' comment if I ever heard one."

Yara slows down chewing her bagel and passes me my coffee. I take it from her and set it on the side table. I crave the warmth and the smell, but my stomach's not feeling up for it quite yet. There's a whole lot of nausea going on in this belly of mine. Yara swallows.

"What else did you guys talk about? And did you use a condom?"

"I don't think so. Last night, I didn't care. I mean, he's been my best friend since college. Last night, I couldn't believe it was finally happening." There's a loose thread protruding from the paisley pink and green quilt that covers

Yara's bed, and I pick at it. "He asked if we should go get the morning-after pill." The thread snaps, leaving a minuscule hole in her quilt. "I said no. My period tracker. I mean, I knew I was safe, but there was something about him asking me that question that just hurt." I lift my head and look at Yara. She's stopped eating and is staring at me. "He was being responsible. It shouldn't hurt me." I fall back onto her pillow and stare at the circular ceiling light.

"And why no morning-after pill?"

I flip my phone over to show her the squares on the period tracker. "It's not the right time."

"I'm not sure I'd trust that." She's staring at it like it's moldy food.

"Catholics around the world do."

"Yeah, and they're notorious for large families."

"Not anymore."

"Yeah, that's because they use birth control now."

I close my eyes. Done with this conversation.

"Oh, Mags. You've been wanting this for years. What else did he say?"

"Nothing. I got dressed and left before he could say anything else."

Yara takes another bite of her bagel. Then she opens the bag, pulls out the remaining buttered bagel, unwraps the silver foil, and passes it to me.

We sit there on her bed. Yara watches over me with a solemn expression as I consume the greasy buttered bagel.

My phone vibrates, and Yara leans forward to read the incoming text message. She passes the phone to me. "Someone's worried about you."

Jason? I lurch forward way too fast, and my throbbing head rebels. I snatch the phone from her.

Dave - TNT
Missed you this morning. All okay?

I toss the phone down on the bed with a grunt. It's a guy from our team. Every year, I choose a Team in Training event to raise money to fight cancer. This year, I'm training for a century ride in Ireland. The event isn't until the spring of next year, though, so I have plenty of time. Our group just met up to start training two weeks ago. This guy, like me, has done several of these events.

This morning, however, was not a training morning. There was no way on god's green earth I was riding twenty miles on my bike this morning. I stare at the dark glass screen with a mild degree of trepidation, as if it might eviscerate me, then pick it back up and scroll through my texts, double-checking that there are no other new ones, then toss it on the bed and lie back down.

"So, what's your next step with Jason?"

"I don't know. Just wait and see what he does? I've wanted this for so long, but in my dreams, the morning after was good and normal. We'd stay in bed and hang out together for the day. It wasn't supposed to feel weird."

"And it did?"

I exhale loudly and rest my arm across my forehead to block the sun. "So weird."

In her chipper, hopeful, too-loud-for-my-pounding-head voice, Yara says, "Well, maybe there's just gonna be an adjustment period? You know? Like, maybe some time is needed for it to sink in, and then you'll both realize this is the natural progression for your relationship. By this weekend, you guys will be one of those couples who are basically living together."

I lift my arm and scowl at her as she reads on her phone. "You think?"

"Well, yeah. It could happen. You two should be together. Everyone assumes you're together. You already get couple-invited everywhere."

"What does that mean?"

"It means that no one invites you without assuming he might come too. And vice versa. You've been coupled for years. I've met people who were shocked to find out you guys were just friends."

"Me too." Nothing new there. I stay over at his place all the time. One of his neighbors came out in the hall one morning exclaiming, "Busted you!" Yeah, yeah. People might not believe me, but we're as platonic as platonic can be. Or at least we were until last night. He just doesn't see me that way. To Jason, I'm good ol' Mags. I search my hazy memory, trying to remember what the heck happened last night that had him kissing me and us getting naked. Tequila. *Why on Earth did we do shots?*

Yara taps my leg to get my attention. "Hey, Jason's an idiot if he tries to keep this in the friend zone. But if he does, you should consider Dave."

"The TNT guy?" Yara nods. She met him when my team gathered at The Dead Poet, a small Irish pub, for beers one day after work. He's nice. He's raising money for cancer research—of course, he's nice. "But don't you think I should wait and see how things work out with Jason? I mean, I know nothing is really going to happen. He doesn't see me that way. But...just in case I'm wrong. I should give it at least this week, right?"

"Yes." Yara talks to me without glancing up from her phone. "That's the plan. You'll see how things go this week with Jason. But if he makes it clear he's all about the friend zone, then next weekend, you are going to ask out Dave."

I eyeball her, not sure I'm liking her plan at all. She holds her hand up to stop an argument that's not even coming out of my mouth. "You can ask him for drinks after work. Keep it casual. You do the casual friend thing better than anybody."

Great. I sit up and drink my lukewarm coffee. "At least there's something I do best."

She lets out a half-laugh while scrolling the captivating device in her hand.

"Jason's going to want to still be just friends, isn't he?"

She doesn't say a word, transfixed by news, or maybe Instagram, but she does reach over to squeeze my hand.

"Shit. What if last night screws up our friendship?" A sense of dread now mingles with nausea.

"There's no way. The two of you have been through hell together. More than once. It might be awkward for a while, but there's no way one night of drunken sex is going to ruin your friendship."

I curl up into a ball on my side as I nibble on my bagel, hoping with all my being that Yara's right on this one. Jason's my best friend. I don't want to lose him.

She slides off the bed to go to the bathroom and pauses at the door.

"What I find shocking is that it's taken this long for the two of you to do the deed. It was bound to happen at some point. Now it's behind you. If anything, it's gonna deepen your friendship. *If* the two of you aren't dating by the end of this week, which I still maintain might happen."

She's got her hand on her hip and waves her index finger at me, all boss-like.

OK, Yara.

three

Jason

The Day We Met

The first time I parked in the Norris Cotton Cancer Center parking lot, the whole moment felt surreal. A referral to an oncologist. What college student needs an oncologist? *I have an appointment with an oncologist* is about as unexpected out of a college student's mouth as *Oh, yes, I know him. He's my cardiologist.*

The imposing white building, accented with green, looks like any hospital. A big asphalt parking lot surrounds the building, with ten handicapped parking spots near the front entrance and an American flag on a towering stainless steel pole.

When I first got the diagnosis, I did some online research. The Dartmouth Medical Center is respected. No reason to travel far to other doctors. At least not based on what I knew at that time.

An elderly volunteer behind a desk greeted people who didn't know where to go. Her smile brought back memories of my grandmother. And a yearning for my parents. I pushed that down and found my way to the correct waiting room.

The waiting room for my doctor looked like any other. Uncomfortable matching chairs with small tables holding stacks of magazines. I signed in with the woman behind the window and sat down in a chair beside a table. The magazine selection sucked. That's when I noticed the girl sitting a couple of chairs away focused on her Kindle.

At first, I wanted to ask her about the electronic device. They were kind of new at the time, and I wanted to know how she liked it. But she never looked up. So, I watched her.

Her dark-brown hair fell around her shoulders, partially covering her face. She wore a black dress—or maybe it's called a jumper—but it was short and fell mid-thigh, exposing lean, long, toned legs. She wore ankle boots with worn brown leather. The toes of the boots were a lighter color as if they'd been worn a lot. An oversized black cardigan hid her arms and chest. She laughed at something in her book, and that was when I noticed the shine of her lip gloss. She had this girl-next-door vibe.

She shifted in her seat. It wasn't until she adjusted her legs that I saw her brown leather slouchy bag below her chair. The Dartmouth button on the strap was my first clue that we shared something in common.

She raised her head, and I pointed to her bag. "You go to Dartmouth?"

Her pale pink lips spread into a friendly, warm smile. "Yes. You?"

"Freshman."

She startled me when she stood, picked up her bag, and sat beside me. The two of us were the only ones in the waiting room. We could have continued our conversation sitting a few seats apart. It was a waiting room, after all. Cordial, distant conversation would have exceeded all social expectations.

After getting situated in the seat directly beside mine, she continued to smile. "What's your major?"

Yes, we sat in an oncology waiting room, and she asked about my major. "Undecided."

"Me too." She glanced down the hall, as if searching for someone, then returned her attention to me.

We talked about classes, dorms, and our upcoming first New Hampshire winter. Being from Missouri, she wasn't too worried. Same for me, since I grew up in Connecticut.

I almost asked her for her number that day. She kept talking and laughing, and I sat there, entranced. She had this healthy glow. Maybe it was just her sun-kissed tan. It was late fall and not that warm, but she looked like someone who spent a lot of time outside. She had a light sprinkling of freckles dusting her cheekbones. Freckles scatter across my entire body, over pale skin, so I always notice freckles.

She talked about missing her parents. She never asked me if I missed mine. If she had, I would've told her I missed them more than she could ever imagine. If I would've answered honestly, which I doubt I would have.

She didn't press me with questions. It made the conversation easy. I had this feeling she and I were going to be friends. Right when I got around to pulling out my phone so I could tap in her number, a nurse with wire-rimmed spectacles stood before us.

"Mr. Longevite?"

Yeah, lady. I'm as shocked as you are that I'm here right now.

Before following the nurse down the hallway, I turned back to the brown-eyed, sun-kissed girl. "Nice to meet you, Maggie. Hope to see you around."

It wasn't until I was down the hall that I worried about her. We didn't ask each other why we were sitting in an oncology waiting room. I remember thinking *if she's here for cancer, please let her kind be totally beatable.*

four

Maggie

Monday morning, I'm sitting at my desk, tapping away on my keyboard, working on a grant. The weekend passed with radio silence from Jason. I could have reached out, and probably should have, but I didn't know what to say. And, given his silence says a whole lot about his thoughts on what happened, then some space is good. Good because when we do speak, I need to squelch these emotions and play it cool. Our friendship is what's most important, and I can't lose sight of that.

There's a tap on my door, and when I glance away from my monitor, I stand so abruptly my chair goes flying backward into the wall.

"What's wrong?"

Therese's clutching a tissue, dabbing her flushed, blotchy, wet cheeks. We work together at The McLoughlin Charity, and both of us also volunteer at a nearby hospice center. We find ourselves holding back tears many times a day. We thrive on knowing we are helping others, but that doesn't make our work any easier. Today, though, Therese isn't keeping her emotions in check. Something serious has happened.

She steps into my office and blows her nose. The sound is muffled, and I grab the tissue box off my desk and take it to her. "Therese?"

"I just got a call from hospice. Johnny." Her lips bunch up, more tears fall, and I pull her into my arms and rub her back. She doesn't need to say anything else. Patients in hospice don't have a lot of time left. We know this when we meet them. And, usually, we do a good job of helping them live while they can and face what's about to happen. We do this and find the joy in being there for them in their last days. And yes, there is joy in those last days. So many times, there's so much love. We're all going to die. Some of us just have a more definitive timeline than others. But there's something about seeing family and friends come together. My personal favorite is when I hear laughter. And the sharing of memories. The love, at times, is almost tangible.

Life is temporary for all of us, but when faced with the end is when it seems we value it most. That's one thing spending time in both a hospital and hospice has given me. An awareness of the importance of living in the moment, of being present. Appreciating all the small things, the everyday normal. Life is too short to live for trips or celebrations. As my grandmother used to say, life's too short to only break out the fine china on holidays. Hospice reminds me every day is the day you should use the china you like best.

Therese agrees. Even so, sometimes the wall protecting our heart from the accompanying sadness of a life ending crumbles, especially when the patient hasn't yet lived a full life. It's tough when the whole entire situation is tragic.

Johnny entered hospice at age seven. His death hits too close to home for Therese because she lost one of her daughters when she was around the same age.

Therese clings to me, sniffling, doing her best to pull it together. She needs this moment to break down, to let some of the emotion out.

"Hey, why don't I take your shift this evening, huh?"

She grabs a fresh tissue and dabs her face. "Yeah? You're not volunteering at Bellevue tonight?"

"Not tonight." I volunteer sporadically at the hospital, sometimes popping in to see if any kid is alone and up for a game.

"I might call Dr. Joyner and see if she has any openings. I feel like things are building up." I nod in understanding. When emotions swirl, they can weigh us down. Make us feel like we're drowning. Sometimes we just have to open up and talk about it. Drain the overflow before it becomes too much. Dr. Joyner is a therapist we both see, although I don't go to see her as frequently as Therese. Therese is broken-hearted over Johnny, but there are other sources for the tidal flow of emotions cascading through her right now. I get it.

I pull her back into my arms for another hug as Jason steps into the office doorway holding a white bakery box. I watch him over Therese's shoulder then squeeze her tight and step back. He lifts the box slightly, a silent offering.

Our New York offices consist of a suite in an office building on the Upper West Side. We're not that close to Columbia, where Jason works, but he walks here all the time. As an assistant professor, he has considerable flexibility in his hours.

The movement captures Therese's attention. She sniffles and smiles.

"Jason. Hi." She swipes at the tears on her cheeks. "Thanks, Mags." The corners of her lips turn up into a sad smile. "I'll leave you two. Good to see you, Jason."

Jason stands to the side of the office door, his chestnut hair a disheveled mess, awkwardly holding out the white box like a peace offering. A sense of relief fills me. He's here. I can't help but notice the wrinkled lines on the corners of his eyes. He looks older...tired.

"Did you bring me doughnuts?"

He opens the box top, displaying half a dozen doughnuts. Half have blue icing, and half have chocolate icing. "I didn't know what kind of mood you'd be in."

I step around him and close my office door for privacy, then take a seat in one of the black plastic scoop chairs in front of my desk while gesturing for Jason to take the other seat. He sets the box on my desk and sits down. He's wearing a slightly rumpled, blue pin-striped dress shirt, black dress slacks, and bright blue running shoes with orange laces. I fully expect he's the most popular professor at Columbia just because he has this way of dressing with a twist. At first glance, he could pass for any other businessman, but then you take that second look and see so much more. He's always wearing running shoes. And he has floppy, coppery hair and freckles that almost blend into each other, and his rugged, square jaw. He's got a short beard right now, but his facial hair is in a constant state of evolution. In a week or two, he'll shave it off, and within a day, he'll sport the gruff, unshaven look.

Over the years, I've had friends tell me that he doesn't have much of a personality, and I can't for the life of me understand why they would think that. He doesn't like to talk much, and often bears a somber expression, but his pale skin unmasks his emotions. He flushes red when angry or excited or amused. He might be guarded, but he's enormously sensitive and vulnerable. And right now, that vulnerability is abundantly evident. His tawny irises flick around the room, tentative, and his right thumb and index finger tap his leg. In the last sixty seconds, he's crossed an ankle over his leg and put it back down on the floor multiple times.

I sit up, cross my legs, and wait. I could make this easy on him, make him feel at home, but I need to know what he's thinking. Something big happened between us, and if I jump to conclusions, I might throw away any chance for more.

He pushes the doughnut box toward me. He seems sad, apologetic, and uncertain. "Doughnut?" His sweet gesture softens the harder feelings I'd been holding in. Any anger or hurt I'd bottled up diminishes. I sit on my hands to prevent jumping out of my chair and wrapping him in a hug.

I shake my head. I do appreciate the gesture, but I don't want a doughnut. He looks down at the floor. He brought me doughnuts. I should drop this. Let it go. But I can't.

"So, you bring doughnuts to all the girls after you sleep with them and don't call?"

His head snaps up, and his pale cheeks flush crimson. "Mags. It wasn't…" He runs his hand through his hair and stands, then paces back and forth in my office. He stops and stands before me with his hands shoved in his pockets. "I didn't know what to say. I should have reached out this weekend. I just…that night…it just…"

"It just what?"

"It shouldn't have happened."

I close my eyes for a moment. Of course, that's how he

feels. He doesn't see me as anything more than a friend. I'm not his type. I know this. I exhale and smile up at him. "Yeah, how did we get so drunk? Crazy, right? I was so hungover on Saturday. Sunday too. Two-day hangover. Unreal—" He bends down, and his hand on my knee shuts me up.

"Are we okay? We gotta be okay, Mags," he pleads. He's as torn up as I am over this, only he's worried solely about our friendship. I'm the one who has been hoping. A low amount of hope, though. Miniscule, really. If he wanted more, he would have acted differently the morning after. He would have called or texted.

"We're good. Let us never speak about it again."

He sits down and holds out his hand with a relieved smile. "Shake on it. Never again."

"Yep. Never again," I mutter as I get up, ignoring his extended hand, and round my desk to sit in my seat. "Now that we've put this behind us, get on out of here. I'm sure you've got papers to grade or students to tutor or something."

I tap at a few keys on my keyboard to bring up some research I had found to reference in the grant I'm in the middle of working on.

He raps my desk with his fist. "I can see you're busy, so I'll go. Want to get together after work? Grab dinner? Your pick."

Me picking sort of goes without saying. He always makes me pick, and I sit there making suggestions until his facial reaction communicates positive receptivity. A fun little "guess what Jason's in the mood for" game we play.

"I can't. I'm volunteering tonight."

"You do Tuesday and Thursday evenings," he says in a questioning tone.

"Tonight I'm covering for Therese. We had a patient pass away, and she's sort of torn up over it. That's what she was upset about."

"She was upset?"

I glance up and notice the crimson shade has spread to his ears. "What?"

"I wish you wouldn't put yourself through that."

"Through what?" This is not a new argument. I know what he's going to say. I shouldn't have even responded to him.

"You've got to move past Adam."

My mouth gapes open, and I breathe through it as I struggle for ample oxygen. That's something he has never, ever said to me before. "What are you talking about?"

He stands over my desk, his hands balled into fists, his neck now red too. Holy shit. Not only is he serious, but he's also emotional.

To get clarification, I ask, "You think I volunteer at a hospice center because I'm not over Adam?"

He stares back, silent, but the muscles in his jaw visibly flex as he grinds his teeth.

"Seriously? That's what you think? Jason. He died twelve years ago."

"Yes. And you are still mourning him. I think you should consider seeing a therapist."

My fingers clench the armrests to stop myself from leaping out of my seat in frustration. I could throttle him. "Me? Me? I should see someone? I do see a therapist. I love going to my therapist. I don't believe I could be in my line of work unless I did talk it out with someone regularly. But what about you? Have you ever seen a therapist, Jason? Ever?"

He thrusts his hands into his pants pockets and glares at me, his lips protruding almost in a pout. It would be cute except he's being such an ass. We glare at each other until his shoulders collapse.

"I'm worried about you. It has to be so hard on you to grow close to people and lose them. I know what you went through. And I worry about you."

All my anger dissipates. Within seconds, I'm around my desk and we're holding each other, and he kisses the top of my head the way he loves to do, in a big brother way.

"I love you, Mags. I want you to be happy."

I breathe him in. His woodsy, earthy, familiar scent.

"I love you too." So much. He wants me to get over Adam. He's so clueless. It's not Adam I need to move past. It's him.

five

Jason

Support Group Day

Fifteen identical chairs created a circle, and the therapist sat in one, sipping his coffee.

I sat in one of the plastic chairs as far away from any other participant as possible. Pushed it out of the chair-made circle, creating an amorphous shape. Other people milled around the coffee table. Some talked to one another in low, discreet voices. Most of the people in the room were middle-aged. The only guy about my age dropped into the chair next to mine.

He smiled. He didn't offer his hand. You 'didn't do that in this group. Fear of germs and all. But he smiled and seemed friendly enough. "Hey, I think you're in my psych class."

"Dartmouth?"

"Yep."

He had short brown hair. A skinny guy. He looked familiar.

"Hauser?"

"Yep. I like him. Even though his TA gives more lectures than he does."

The therapist at the front of the room spoke up to start the session. "Welcome. This is our support group for those battling a disease. Many here have cancer, but not all. We start out each session with a little check-in, going around the room and letting everyone introduce themselves and maybe mention how things are going. If you've got any good news or bad news, this would be the time to share it. Then we'll move on to discussions." He paused and tapped the toe of his shoe on the vinyl flooring.

"Before we begin, I'd like to remind you, everyone here is in a similar situation. At home, you may feel you need to guard what you say for the sake of your loved ones. You may not want them to worry. Here, there is no need to guard what you say. There is no need to protect the person you are talking to. This is your space and time to share how you really feel. To put those emotions out there. Now, who would like to start?"

A bald man sitting two empty chairs away from the therapist raised his hand. His light brown cardigan reminded me of Mr. Rogers from the kids' TV show.

"Okay, Howard. Please introduce yourself."

Tears streamed down the man's face. I was sitting pretty far away from the guy, but I could see the tears. The man started sniffling before he ever spoke. Some folks looked down at the ground, and one old lady leaned forward in her chair, as if by leaning closer she'd do something for him. The guy mumbled stuff, but between his tears, you couldn't understand him.

The whole situation was weird. My oncologist encouraged me to come to this group. Maybe he didn't know the average age of folks who attended group therapy. I wanted to laugh. Clearly an inappropriate reaction, but it was so awkward. *Howard, man, get it together.*

I stood to make my way to the coffee table. Moving around probably violated group therapy behavior etiquette, but it was too uncomfortable. Too weird. The guy was crying buckets before he even said his full name.

I pumped coffee out of one of the stainless steel dispensers, cursing myself for showing up for what appeared to be some sort of adult version of Camp Kumbaya, but instead of telling scary stories around a campfire, each person took turns crying.

The guy from my psych class came up beside me. "Wanna get out of here?"

I set my coffee down on the table, pointed toward the door and mouthed, "Let's go."

We both speed-walked out of that church basement room faster than two girls walking to lose weight. It wasn't until we were on the sidewalk outside the church that we both busted out laughing.

"Howard, dude!" the brown-haired guy shouted, clutching his side from laughing so hard.

"That shit's supposed to make you feel better? I thought someone in there was going to slice a wrist."

"Right? I know. Fuck. Hey, my name's Adam. What's yours?" Then he stuck his hand out to shake mine. I'd just met the guy, but I knew if he was in that room, he probably had something that meant he shouldn't be shaking hands during flu season. But he looked alive. Vibrant. And I shook his hand.

"My girlfriend's studying tonight. You want to go grab dinner?"

We left the quack session and went out for burgers and beer with our fake IDs. We talked about a lot of nothing. He told me about his girlfriend, this amazing girl he met during orientation. When he found out I wasn't dating anyone, he kept pointing out girls, asking if I'd want to meet *that* one. I'd shove his hand down so the girl wouldn't see him pointing. A subtle wingman, Adam was not.

Thinking back, that night sort of started it all.

six

Maggie

There is always a sense of something missing after a patient passes. It hits me the second I step onto the floor, a sense as I wander down the hall that the patient is with me, watching the activity in the hall. A sensation that the soul is yearning to reach out and hug those of us who feel his absence. Or maybe he's hanging back to see what kind of food has been mangled by the cafeteria today or who's going to get the extra cup of Jell-O. Whatever the reason, it feels like the soul lingers.

This evening is no different. I pause in the doorway of room 333, and sadness flows through me like an ebbing tide. I'm told I just missed Johnny's mom.

Sadness permeates the hall and infiltrates the crevices. When a life ends, it hurts. Our days are numbered. It's true for every single soul blessed with the miracle of life.

There's a song out that I love. The singer wishes his loved

one pain. I think he's actually talking to his child. It doesn't matter who he's talking to. His point is a good one. Pain allows us to more deeply appreciate our time on this Earth. If we lived life in a magical place—say, a Garden of Eden for all—where there is no pain or suffering and food is plentiful, would we fully appreciate a crisp, fresh apple? If we could live forever, would we waste our days?

Obviously, I don't know for sure. But I suspect it's the disappointments and losses in life, the challenges, that at the end of the day, truly make it worth living. Volunteering at the hospital and hospice remind me to cherish life. And I enjoy knowing that I'm making a positive difference for someone currently experiencing so much pain. Either the patient or the loved one. The pain hits both.

I'm putting away the craft cart for the night when Gloria comes up behind me. "You know, your gentleman friend is waiting in the lobby for you." I can't help but smile at how she describes Jason.

"Jason's here?"

"You got any other gentleman friends hanging around?" She holds the closet door open for me, waiting for me to finish up. I dump the remaining mints from a bowl into a plastic bag. They're individually wrapped, but leaving them out in a bowl on the craft cart overnight grosses me out. I don't like to think of them getting dusty or attracting ants or who knows what.

"No other gentleman friends. But you know, Ms. Halloway, like I've told you before, I don't think Jason meets your criteria of a gentleman friend."

"Uh-huh," she responds in a deep, drawn-out tone with a mischievous smile.

I roll my eyes and step out of the closet. "Where is he?"

"Downstairs in the lobby. By the main entrance."

"Have a goodnight, Ms. Halloway."

"You too, sweetie."

The elevator doors open, and I head out into the lobby. Visiting hours are over at nine p.m. It's not exactly packed, like, say, at rush hour on the subway platform, but there's a noticeable uptick in the number of people passing through the lobby. Jason's sitting by himself on the pleather sofa, one ankle resting on his knee as he flips through a *Sports Illustrated* magazine that someone left behind on the side table. This hospice subscribes to a number of publications, but I don't know why. It seems people are always leaving magazines on the tables in the lobby. It's a good pass it forward, do something good for the world kind of thing.

I stand a few feet in front of him and observe. Under the fluorescent lights, his reddish hair has glints of a brighter, coppery shade. His shoulders slouch down and inward in this way that he has as if he's carrying a great weight and it's all he can do to remain upright. Understandably, he hates hospitals of any sort, and he shouldn't be here. That thought has me striding over at a quick pace and kicking his running shoe that's flat on the ground.

Startled, his head lurches up. He smiles until my harsh words hit him. "What're you doing here?"

He drops the magazine on the table and shoves his hands into his pockets, sheepish. "I thought this evening might be tough for you. I figured you might need a friend."

Right. A friend. "Come on, let's go. You have dinner yet?"

"Yeah." It's after nine p.m. Of course he has. "Want to get a beer? Or we could head back to my place and watch TV. Anything you want. Something to take your mind off things, you know."

We turn right out of the Hospice of New York building and automatically head to his apartment. He's talking about taking my mind off hospice. He always acts like it hurts me. He's my best friend, but he doesn't get me. He doesn't understand that I love helping out here and in the hospital.

He also doesn't get that a lot of the time when I seem sad, it's because of him. For years, I've wanted more with him. And I've settled, simply happy to be with him. Happy to be there for him. But I'm almost thirty-two. And I get that he'll never see me that way. He'll never see me as anything other than Adam's girl. Maybe by now he even sees me as a little sister. After all, I'm probably the closest thing he has to family.

As we stroll down the sidewalk, he drapes his arm around my shoulders, and I wrap my arm around his waist. It's our walking embrace that somehow developed over time. I fit perfectly under his arm. I especially love when we do this at the end of a long day. Having him close is like a balm on sunburn. Soothing.

He stops in the middle of the city sidewalk. We're on a side street, between the avenues, and it's not super busy, but I do notice one man grumble as he passes us. Then he tilts my head up, and the rest of the world fades to black. My breath catches, and my chest tightens in anticipation beneath his intense gaze. His lips are inches from mine. His thumb strokes my chin. I lean forward, holding my breath, as his face inches closer. Ready.

"Are you sure you're okay?" In the space of a nanosecond, he's a foot away with both hands shoved in his pockets.

I close my eyes to hide my emotions. I've got to stop this. He's not going to try to kiss me. Not when he's sober. He sees me as a friend.

There's a saying that only an insane person does the same exact thing time and time again and expects a different result. Well, I don't expect a different result. I hope for a different result. Does that make me a little less insane?

Time to stop hoping. When I open my eyes, his dark orbs peer back through a squint, deepening his crow's feet, evidence of his concern. I shift and push forward, one foot in front of the other.

"Yes. I wish you'd listen to me. I'm good."

"Well, if you're all good, maybe I'll pick the TV show."

I shove him to the side, and he nearly rams a teenager rambling down the sidewalk with white earbuds jammed in his ears. The distracted guy dips to the side, barely registering his near hit. Jason pushes me back, and we both slip into our soft shove on the sidewalk game, chuckling as we go in the sophomoric, Beavis and Butthead kind of way we have.

The last thing my almost thirty-two-year-old self needs to be doing is going back to his house for a beer and TV watching. I should tell him no. Text Yara and meet up with her. Or text that TNT guy and see what he's up to. That's what I should do. But what will I do? Yep. I'll keep walking with him straight back to his place. Because that's what I do.

seven

. . .

Jason

The Day We All Met

I saw her first. Sitting in the quad, in front of the library.

You might not know this, but that library, the Baker-Berry Library, is ranked as one of the most beautiful university libraries in the country. It is. There's this huge lawn in front of it. Designed to mimic the Independence Hall in Philadelphia, it's impressive. Memorable. It's one of the things that attracted me to the school when I did my first campus visit. But it's nothing compared to Maggie. I know, it's a nonsensical comparison.

But, if you could have seen her that spring day, out on the lawn. Standing beside a blanket spread out on the grass, surrounded by a couple of girlfriends. Laughing, the sunlight reflecting along her hair, shimmering like the surface of a lake on a summer day. She looked carefree. Happy. Really, she's like that on almost any day, but this particular day, it's timestamped in my memory. When I'm lying on my deathbed, I'm going to close my eyes and remember how she looked that day.

I stood there on the lawn, near a tree, watching her from afar, in shock we'd crossed paths once again. I'd figured the best I could hope for would be to have her in a class next semester. I kept an eye out for her everywhere I went. Even when I spent time in the hospital, I remained watchful.

And on that random Tuesday, I found her. Wearing cut-off denim shorts, a big burgundy sweatshirt, and Uggs. Her faint tan highlighted the muscular lines of her long legs. Her hair spilled over and around her hoodie.

I don't know why I stood there for so long, watching her. Like a creeper. I guess maybe trying to figure out how to approach her. What to say. But, as I stood there, frozen, Adam walked up.

Since that day at the whacked group counseling session, Adam and I, well, we'd hung out some. Even ended up in the hospital together for a brief bout with high fevers. He'd come to Dartmouth to play lacrosse, but he couldn't play this year. He'd been diagnosed with Hodgkin's the year before starting school. We didn't talk much about cancer and all that stuff. But he served as my guide to all things cancerous. I got my diagnosis after school started.

Since we had the same kind of cancer, if I had questions, I'd text him. He'd been through radiation. My plan was to tackle a full course that coming summer. Adam was the only person on campus who knew what I had. It wasn't something I wanted stamped on my head everywhere I went, so I kept it quiet. No one on campus knew except Adam. I liked hanging out with him because I could just be. No hiding. At that point in time, we shared perspectives on the world. Cancer sucked. Bad grade on a test? Who cared? Bigger things to stress about. Pity? We didn't want it. We had one script for cancer-free friends, one script for friends like us. Out of everyone, Adam knew me best.

So, imagine my surprise when he looped his arm around Maggie and brushed a quick kiss across her lips. It felt like someone sucker-punched me. *Boom.*

Then the pieces fell in place. That day at the oncologist, she'd been waiting for him. It had to be. He'd mentioned once that he had a girlfriend. He'd said she'd been awesome during his treatment. Told me I was smart to be going back to Texas. Said I wouldn't want to be alone during all that.

Adam saw me before she did. "Hey, man." Adam seemed to know everyone on campus. Outgoing. Charismatic. The kind of guy you'd expect to be both class president and vale-dictorian. A born leader.

"Hey. How goes it?" I was trying to be casual, cool. Not give away that I was reeling from figuring out my girl crush and his girlfriend were one and the same.

She looked up to see who Adam was talking to, and her whole face brightened as she smiled. Genuine happiness. Her girlfriends waved goodbye, and she joined us.

"Hey! There you are. You took off for your appointment without us exchanging contact info." Then she tugged on Adam's shirt. "This is the guy I told you about. The Dart-mouth student I met in the waiting room." Adam sat down, and she did too, close to him, touching him. Books were spread out on the blanket.

Turning his attention to me, he welcomed me in that Adam way. No one was ever unwelcome with Adam. "Come on, sit down, and join us. Gorgeous day." He toyed with her hair with one hand while directing me to a spot on the blanket with the other.

I had a few hours before my last class of the day. A lab of some sort. I sat down on the edge of the blanket. We talked.

We exchanged numbers, Maggie and I. Adam and I already had each other's numbers. By virtue of knowing Adam, without me saying anything, she knew what I was going through. Even back then, she knew what I needed before I did. And by virtue of being Adam's friend, I became the recipient of her friendship.

Without a doubt, if you are the recipient of Maggie's friendship, you are one lucky, lucky human being. She's truly such a caring person, it's unreal. She cares deeply. And, there's nothing in this world like being her friend. The whole campus knew it too. Everybody loved Maggie.

After that day and hanging out on the blanket for that couple of hours, I kind of became their third wheel. And I was in a weird place, waiting for the academic year to end so I could follow this course mapped out for me to kill the cancer. My oncologist was optimistic. No one seemed super worried. But I didn't want to talk about it. So, it wasn't like I was reaching out and trying to make new friends. Maggie and Adam knew. They always invited me to places. So, if I was up for it, I went. Lunch. Dinner. Beers. Library. By the time we wrapped up freshman year, they were without a doubt my two closest friends. Adam and Maggie.

eight

Maggie

Jason has this incredibly deep, soft, plush sofa. I still remember the day we picked it out. We were standing in the middle of this massive furniture store, people milling all around, and he spread out across it, shoes and all. I screeched, "Your shoes!"

He gave me his usual smile, the smallest of smiles others don't usually see. Tugging on my hand, he pulled me down beside him. Spooning, he whispered into my ear, "Let's make sure this works before we do this."

I thought my heart was going to explode within my chest. Yes, we often end up like this at the end of movie nights. We'll start the evening out on opposite ends and somehow, he'll stretch out, and then I'll stretch, and then he'll slide in behind me so his feet aren't in my face. It's my absolute favorite way to fall asleep.

The salesperson came up and assumed we were a couple.

She walked right up to us, overlooked our shoes lying on the floor model, and said, "Looks like we have a winner."

Tonight, Jason and I find ourselves spooning once again. His leg has found a way between mine, and there's a blanket over us. His hand rests on my hip, and every now and then his breath flutters across my ear. I lost focus on the show ages ago. Of course, Jason is entranced by the movie. I shift my hips back against him, without intent, as I squeeze my thighs together. My movement is subtle, but strong, teasing my core.

Then I hear it. A low, guttural moan. I roll my hips back again, and I shift because I'm almost positive he has an erection pressed against me. But he doesn't see me that way, does he?

I roll my body back, just enough that I can look up at him. He strokes along my stomach, below my shirt on my bare skin. Time crawls to a stop. This is the moment when it's all going to change. He's going to kiss me. And we're both sober. This is the moment when our friendship grows into something more.

Those hypnotic chestnut irises draw me in. I reach up, and ever so softly, my thumb scrapes the line of his rough chiseled jaw, then my fingers graze his coppery strands. His lips are inches from mine, and his breath is shallow. I stretch, flexing against him.

Without warning, he jerks off the sofa onto his feet, and I land with a thud on the floor.

"Shit, sorry."

I now have a clear view of the underside of his coffee table. He extends a hand to help me up. So, no kiss, then. I shouldn't expect more. Shouldn't get my hopes up. I know better. I pull my legs under me and decline his hand, using the coffee table as support to push myself up. I keep my head down, gaze riveted to the floor, avoiding Jason. My cheeks radiate heat.

His face flushes red. Anger? Embarrassment? That's the thing with a redhead, or ginger, as I like to call him. I know he's affected; his pale skin color reveals that much. What's running through his mind? As well as I know him, I can't always tell.

"It's late. I should get outta here." I exhale loudly and pat my jeans down, all the while visually inspecting the frayed knotted rug on his floor.

"Maggie." He says my name with a pleading sound as if he's begging me for something.

He stands two feet in front of me, gazing down at me with a sympathetic expression. I'm not sure how he's feeling, but I am most definitely embarrassed. I charge to the door, grab my pocketbook, then lean down to pull on my boots. The pocketbook strap trails off my arm and crashes against the wall.

He reaches down and picks it up. He stands there, patiently waiting, silent, as I pull on my boots. I reach for my pocketbook, but he holds it higher in the air, away from me.

"Maggie, you know I love you, right?"

"Yes."

"We can't. We can't go there. You're my best friend. I can't lose you. And we haven't talked about it. Not really. But we can't have a repeat of what happened the other night. You understand that, right?"

"Yes. You don't think of me that way. I'm like—"

"Wait. You think I don't think of you like that? I'm alive, Maggie. Hell, every guy on the planet who sees you thinks of you like that. But, Maggie," he reaches out and tugs on my chin, forcing me to look up, "you are so much more than that. You deserve more than that. More than what I can give you. You deserve it all. And I just…we just…we gotta hold on to our friendship. I can't let other urges get in the way of that." He stops, scratches his beard, and after a pause, lets out a subdued chuckle. "Hell, Adam would kill me. You know that."

Adam. He's the one who will never let him go. And maybe that's what will always be between us. I close my eyes, reeling a bit. A desire to get away from this apartment, away from Jason and his rejection, builds, and I reach for the doorknob. "I understand."

"Maggie," he pleads.

"No worries. I understand. See you tomorrow." I give him my warmest, most comforting smile.

Jason lives two blocks away from me. When we first made plans to move to the city, we did consider moving in together. But, right out of college, my parents pushed for me to find a female roommate. Jason bought the place he's living in, and I found Yara's ad looking for a roommate in a place conveniently close to Jason's. In a little last laugh on my parent's kind of thing, Yara ended up being a lesbian. Her sexuality has never been an issue between us at all. But I did have fun shocking my conservative Midwest parentals with that bit of information.

Sometimes I wonder if I had moved in with him, if my parents hadn't interfered, would we still be in the same situation? Or would the constant proximity in a small city apartment have forced intimacy? One thing's for sure. If we were living together, his apartment would be better decorated.

Every guy on the planet who sees you thinks of you like that. Yet, in the friend's box we remain.

The heavy apartment door shuts behind me as my back pocket vibrates. I pull my phone out and see it's my sister.

"Hey, Zoe."

"How's it going?"

I sigh as I make my way down the city sidewalk, holding my breath as I near a pile of black garbage bags awaiting pickup. A guy on an electric scooter zips by and flashes me a look as if I'm the one who shouldn't be on the sidewalk. Instead of turning onto Manhattan Avenue, I go straight across 116th Street. Morningside Park calls my name.

"Fine," I blurt out.

There's a pause, then with a sarcastic bite that's all Zoe, "Yep. Sounds like it."

Artificial lights shine on the sidewalk and streets, creating a well-lit thoroughfare. There's an empty park bench below a black iron streetlight, and I plop onto it. The quiet abandoned playground reminds me it's late, and climbing the steep park stairs by myself at this time of evening wouldn't be particularly smart. The prospect of going home to face Yara doesn't appeal to me either, though. I've already got Zoe on the phone. I'm not feeling strong enough to take the one-two punch. The silence across the line must tip off my intuitive sister.

"Hey...somethings wrong. What's going on?" Concern drips off her every word.

"Nothing. Nothing at all."

"Is it Jason?"

I nod, fully aware that she can't see me but fairly certain she senses my answer. We live far apart, but we'll always be close.

"Sweetie, one-sided love sucks." The headlights of vehicles passing down Morningside Avenue blur. To hold the pesky tears in, I blink and inhale deeply.

"Come home. At least move to Chicago if Iowa isn't calling to you. It's time. Time to put some space between the two of you."

I barely enunciate the words. "But I love him." Somehow, my sister hears me.

"I know, sweetie. But don't you want more? Someone who loves you fully, the way you deserve to be loved? Kids? He's never gonna give you that. Ever. If it was going to happen, it would have happened by now. I know you love him, but this isn't healthy. You guys slipped past healthy years ago."

Her words are hard to hear, but she says them so softly, and with such tenderness, they feel comforting. I swallow, lift my head to the sky, close my eyes, and ask her about home.

nine

Jason

The Days at Hospice

Adam texted to tell me he'd been admitted to hospice. I'll never forget the day. September. Sophomore year. The temperature high registered a brisk sixty-two degrees.

I'd spent the summer in Texas. Finished chemo. Adam and I texted some. Not much. He'd been a bit MIA as school approached. Nothing unusual for summer break. I knew he and Maggie had driven cross-country. I figured he'd been having an amazing summer. And expected when we got back to school, he, Maggie, and I would hang out some, once we got into a routine, if they felt like having a third wheel. I'd texted him a few times, but he hadn't yet responded. I'd thought he was just busy, getting acclimated to a new year.

The text said to call if I got a chance. He'd like to say

goodbye. Who the fuck sends a text like that? *I'd like to say goodbye.*

I couldn't call him. A phone call felt inadequate. And the last I'd seen him, he'd looked healthy. Healthier than me. He wasn't headed to treatments all summer.

I hopped a plane to California. His roommate gave me his mom's number, and she told me where to find him. From the outside, the building looked like a home with a parking lot. The black asphalt lot that surrounded the building, butting up to the front and sides, was the only element that made it clear it was a business. Well, the asphalt, six handicapped parking spots, and the small rectangular sign that read *Southern California Hospice.*

The wide entry hall opened into an area that felt like a den in someone's home. Comfortable couches and chairs. An empty brick fireplace against one wall. To the far side, a woman sat behind a reception counter. I ignored her, because my gaze fell on Maggie.

I hadn't reached out to her in my rush to get here. Didn't know she'd be here, in California. I mean, it made sense. She'd spent the summer with him.

Seeing her wasn't something I'd prepared for. I was struck by how alone she looked. The brown leather club chair she sat in dwarfed her. Swollen, bloodshot eyes and mottled cheeks. When I approached, she seemed relieved to see a familiar person. She wrapped her arms around me and buried her face against my chest.

Visitors filled Adam's room. His parents, relatives. Probably more than one minister. There was a constant stream of people in and out, producing a low hum of conversation. Most were adults far older than us. Maybe the adults had lived long enough to know what to say.

Because back then, as a college student, I sure as shit didn't know what to say.

When I walked into his room, he looked surprised. Then he grinned. Said something about he should have known when I didn't respond that meant I was on my way.

He looked like an old man in that bed. It's amazing how much cancer ages you towards the end. So thin. Frail. There were no tubes or beeping devices. No. In hospice, all those annoyances are gone. It's peaceful- compared to a hospital. Hospice is all about making the patient comfortable for their last days. It sucked. The whole thing sucked.

Adam's mom. She was nice enough to me. She and his dad let me have a few moments alone with him. She was noticeably colder to Maggie. Adam ignored it, and I didn't blame him. He had enough to deal with without trying to solve some issues between his mom and Mags.

Adam, he was surrounded by people he loved. And every single one of them treated Maggie like they didn't know her. I guess they didn't. She wasn't family. She wasn't from there. Didn't grow up with him. But she loved him. You'd think that would be enough.

Some people were just unaware. Absorbed in the sadness —in the wrongness—of having to say goodbye to a college kid. But there was more there between his mom and her. Since Adam wasn't protecting her, I did. I stood by her.

It'd be great to say Adam and I had some profound exchange. I guess because we both had been facing the same shit, we got each other. From whispered exchanges outside of his room, I gathered that his cancer had spread. Everywhere.

I'd be lying if I said a part of me didn't want to ask about more specifics about his treatment. Make sure my doctor had recommended a different course of action than his had. Find out what he did that didn't work, because there had to be a reason for him to be so sick, right? Somehow his doctor must have screwed up. If we'd been back at school, I probably would have drilled him with questions. But in that room, with him in that bed…no.

I'd like to say we were by his bedside when he passed. But it didn't happen as quickly as they thought. He hung on for several weeks. Maggie and I stayed for a week, but we needed to get back to school. To life. He was asleep a lot, anyway. Drug-induced, probably. But still, his parents encouraged us to go back to school, and we did.

At one point, a rare moment when we were alone, Adam did tell me to look out for Maggie. His exact words were something like, "She may need a friend. She's a good one." He got that last part wrong, though. She's the best.

ten

Maggie

"Earth to Maggie…"

On reflex, my wandering mind returns from people watching along Broadway, and my cheeks warm in embarrassment. I've been staring out the window. When I agreed to meet Dave here, I knew I wouldn't be great company, but I thought we'd be with the Team-In-Training group and I could blend in. As it turns out, I must not've paid attention to his text, and it's just the two of us. I grimace. "Sorry."

"No problem. Everything okay? You look stressed."

"Stuff at work." The red wine he selected has hints of blackberries that linger after each sip. It's a lighter red than the cabernet sauvignon I generally prefer, but I've come to expect that from many of the French wines. Dave commandeered the wine list the minute we sat down. Given Le Pif has close to forty wines by the glass, I had no issue ceding drink selection. This evening, any of the wines on the menu will meet my objective to unwind.

Dave watches me, his arm extended on the table, his hand inches from mine. I rest my elbows on the table and cup the bulb of the wine glass.

"That's a pretty sad face for it to be stuff at work."

For a moment, I study Dave. He's a good-looking guy. Thick, dark blond hair, cut short but long enough that it's a little unruly, and monotone brown eyes. He's tall and lean. I know enough about him to know he's a really good guy. This is his fourth team-in-training fundraiser, and he's already raised over fifteen thousand dollars from family, friends, and businesses for this singular event. As I'm taking him in, it occurs to me I don't know what he does. Our connection has been training.

He reaches out and lightly touches my hand. "Maggie?"

"Sorry." I smile and release the wine glass, place my palms flat on my thighs, and lean back. "My heads just off in la-la land." It's a half-truth. He deserves a better explanation for my absentee behavior. "I keep running through everything I still need to do on a grant application that's due soon."

"Like what?"

"Oh, prove we're doing a good job of managing our finances. That if given the grant, we'll make each dollar go far. This one's asking for more than normal, so I don't have the information at my fingertips. Year-to-date financials. Nothing you want to hear about."

"You guys don't employ an accountant?"

"No. We have six full-time employees. The accountant we use volunteers his time, and he's an executive."

"Well, I'm not an accountant, but I do have a friend who might be willing to help."

"Thanks, but I've got a friend helping me." Said friend just happens to be emotionally unavailable and is the real reason I'm in a funk. It'll pass. It always does. I sense Dave's struggling with something to say, so I help him out by asking him what he does for a living. The conversation tactic works, and he carries the conversation forward. As he's talking, my phone lights up on the table.

> **Jason**
> Want to order from Pasta Fari tonight?

I lift my phone to respond to Jason while nodding and smiling to Dave so he'll know to continue talking.

> **Maggie**
> Can't. Out to dinner.

Three dots come and go, and I listen to Dave while keeping an eye on the dots. Within seconds, his reply appears.

> **Jason**
> With who?

> **Maggie**
> Dave.

This time the dots appear and disappear. Dave has finished talking, so I smile and ask him, "So, where did you say you're from?"

He smiles. "I don't think I did. Minnesota."

"Oh, wow. Do you miss it?"

Jason
Have the numbers to go over with you. Have
some questions.

I push the phone away from me, but have it set where I can see any more texts that come through. Dave leans forward, telling me all about ice fishing.

"You'd love it."

"Sitting on ice? Doesn't particularly sound like my kind of thing."

"We bring chairs. You'd be comfortable. My sisters join us sometimes."

"What about the fish?"

"What do you mean?"

"Isn't it kind of cruel? They're in survival mode, existing in the harshest of temperatures, and they get a glance at food, and then they're pulled up to the surface, and they die." It's awful the more I think about it, about what the fish must be feeling, the excitement and then a painful hook.

"It's not like that. I promise. The fish don't have brains."

He's smiling at me like he thinks I'm being cute. I glance around the place, wishing for some of my teammates. No other conversational cues spring to mind, so I push forward with the distasteful topic at hand.

"Tell me about your best ice fishing trip." He relaxes into his seat and falls into entertainer mode. My heart's not in the conversation, but his willingness to continue talking with the slightest prompt from me is appreciated. If he wasn't so talkative, with the way I'm feeling, we'd be staring at our wine glasses in silence.

Jason
Are you on a date?

My chest freezes. My focus centers around the rectangular device on the table and the words on the screen. Could he be jealous? I'd be a disaster if he were on a date. I snap up my phone to respond.

Maggie
No. Team in Training.

Jason
Come by after?

Maggie
Not sure what time I'll be done.

Jason
Where are you? I can join.

Maggie
Le Pif

Jason
Broadway and 71st?

A sound from across the table distracts me from my text exchange. At some point, Dave stopped talking.

Dave gestures to the phone held tight in my grip. "Work?"

"Yeah. Remember the financial information I need?"

The muscles along his jaw relax, and he sits back in his chair. He has a laidback, easygoing mannerism to him that's appealing.

We're sitting right next to the double doors, and every

time the doors open, a blast of chilly fall air hits me from the back. This time, as the cold air surrounds me, Yara's booming greeting echoes through the wine bar. "Hello!"

I jump off the high chair to greet my roommate with a warm hug. I completely spaced that I had invited her to join us. As I'm sliding my glass over to claim the seat by the window and allow Yara to take my seat, Dave's wide-eyed expression brings me to my senses.

"Dave, you met Yara before, right? At the team happy hour last week? She's my roommate. She comes to a lot of our team social events, even though she has yet to actually train."

Yara smiles and explains, "Well, I'm game for alcohol. Not so much the running or the biking or any of that physical hoopla." She takes a seat, and he shows her the menu, pointing out what we're drinking and telling her about some of the other selections he's had. I pick up my phone to resume my conversation with Jason.

Maggie
Yes, that's the location. Are you coming?

Jason
Almost there.

I offer a polite smile to Dave and Yara as I shimmy off the high stool. Yara gives me a questioning glance, and I gesture to the door, holding up an index finger while mouthing, "Be right back."

Out on the sidewalk, I look up and down Broadway. Pedestrians hustle by while streetlights and lights from the stores and restaurants lining the avenue give the street a late afternoon glow. A man returns to his locked bike, and I watch as he unlocks the massive chain and slips it over his shoulder bike messenger style. A couple enters the Chase Manhattan bank on the corner.

The moment I see Jason's coppery hair bobbing toward me, I wave my hand in the air to get his attention. He smiles when he sees me, and as soon as he's near enough, I'm throwing my arms around him. When he holds me, it's as if his nearness sends a message to my psyche, and my muscles relax, and any heaviness weighing me down slips away. He holds me a tad longer than normal, and his nose dips into my hair. It's this sweet thing Jason does, as if he's captivated by the scent of my hair. When I change shampoos, he'll always comment. It's a quirk of his that I happen to love.

I also love his woodsy scent. He doesn't wear cologne, and I know the scent is from the Tom's of Maine deodorant he uses and maybe also his bath soap. I purchase handmade, all-natural, chemical-free soap for him. I usually select soaps with almost no scent, but sometimes I'll pick out something with a hint of rosemary or cedar. Instinctively, I bury my nose at the base of his neck to breathe him in.

Jason pushes the heavy iron door open for me to pass, then comes up behind me, his arm possessively resting on my lower back as we approach the table. Yara rolls her eyes and sips her wine, barely acknowledging Jason with a slight nod. *Nice, Yara.*

Jason extends his hand and introduces himself to Dave. I squeeze past Yara to get back into my seat by the window. Jason stares at the empty seat across from me. It's a tight fit between Dave and the wall. Yara exhales loudly, dramatically angles her head up to the ceiling, and hops off her chair.

"Sit here," she tells him.

Jason wraps his arm behind the back of my chair as he sits. He isn't exactly outgoing, and I'm not sure when we developed this routine, but him remaining close by my side in social situations is our norm.

Dave isn't smiling. His brow wrinkles, and a deep crevice forms between his eyebrows. All signs of amiable Dave evaporate.

"It's getting late. Why don't I ask for the check?" Dave asks the table but doesn't wait for an answer. He raises his hand, waving it to get the waitress's attention.

Yara taps her fingers on the table and blatantly glares at me. It's awkward, and I kick her under the table in frustration. I'm not exactly sure what her problem is, but she's making the whole situation weird.

Jason, oblivious to any tension, motions Dave off calling the waitress over, telling him, "Don't worry about it. I'll pay for yours when we leave later. Good to meet you, Dave." He nods Dave's way, his version of a goodbye, and with his right arm tucked around the back of my chair, doesn't make any kind of move to extend his hand for a cordial goodbye.

"Are you sure you have to go? Dave and Yara just got here." He'd probably like them both if he got to know them.

"Yeah, this date's not going quite how I thought it would." He throws back the remainder of his wine then reminds me, "Don't drink too much. See you at seven a.m. Fifteen miles."

As soon as he's out the door, Yara slaps my hand.

"You were on a date?" she whisper-shrieks. "You invited us on your date?"

"It wasn't a date. It was supposed to be a group, and only he and I showed up."

"Maggie. He called it a date."

"No, he didn't."

"Yes. He said, 'This *date* isn't going how I thought it would.' What the hell, Mags? You don't invite friends to join you on a date." She's leaning over the table as she says this, her glittery gold eyeshadow sparkling under the overhead pendant light.

Jason smirks, the corners of his lips barely turned up.

"What?" I demand, glaring at him.

He sits straighter in his chair and places both hands in the air in a defensive gesture. "I'm just sitting here."

"It wasn't a date," I mutter under my breath as I toy with the base of my wine glass.

Yara doesn't drop it. Instead, she points at Jason. "You are the reason she's going to end up foregoing her dream of having children. You can't show up on her dates."

"You showed up."

They glare at each other until Yara jumps off her chair. "I'm heading to the restroom. Order me a glass of whatever you're having. Since money bucks over here is paying. That's what you said, right, professor?"

"You walked into that one," I tell him. He'd pay for her drinks anyway—he's gracious like that—but it's still amusing to watch Yara in action.

A serious expression crosses his face. When Jason is serious, his lips form a straight line, and his brow smooths as if every facial muscle has been called to attention. "When we're done here, I need you to come back to my apartment. I've been digging into the Excel sheets you shared. This year is vastly different from the summaries from years past. It might be the limited view I have based on the spreadsheets you have access to, but I have a list of additional information I need, and I need to make sure you understand it."

He's all business and concern. Not about my maybe-date with Dave or Yara's accusation that I'll never have children because of him. But because of the financial status of the not-for-profit I work for. He's a good friend. He cares. And he'll never be anything more than a friend.

eleven

Jason

The Funeral

Every so often, I relive Adam's funeral. I see the day and the people. The service. The priest, or pastor, I don't know what denomination Adam's family followed, but this man in a long black robe stood at the front and shouted at the packed church. "If you want to see Adam again, you will believe in God Almighty. If you want to join Adam at the table of Christ, you will believe." The last word, believe, dragged out, as in 'beleeeeeeve.' Maggie and I shifted on the wooden pew. Tears streaked her face, but at that juncture, both of us strapped down the smiles that wanted to rise. That robed guy was just too over the top, televangelist style.

Adam's parents sat in the family section, to the side of the robed man. His mother stared straight ahead, at times visibly sobbing. His father nodded in agreement at almost every-thing the pastor said. He even nodded when the pastor reminded all of us that "God works in mysterious ways. We cannot question the ways of the Lord."

Of course, science had uncovered lots about cancer. In time, with more research, we'd know a lot more. What caused it, how to cure it.

I wanted to argue with the robed man and try to make him see that we very much did need to question cancer and find solutions. Make him see that science might not have all the answers yet, but that we could make progress if we asked questions and trusted in science. Our knowledge wasn't far enough along to save Adam, but one day, we'd know enough to save a different nineteen-year-old.

Maggie stood graveside after everyone else left. With her head bowed, she stood alone, sobbing. Her back was to me, but every now and then, the wind carried the sounds of her sobs, and her shoulders shook.

Never have I ever felt more helpless. There was nothing I could do. She was heartbroken. And it wasn't just Maggie. It was everyone. That church was packed. It was like every single person Adam went to school with, or played team sports with, or went to camp with, or bumped into line at Starbucks had come to his funeral. So many people, completely crushed over the tragic death.

And I kept thinking, and I know you are going to tell me I shouldn't…that it isn't 'the case. But I kept thinking, it should have been me. We had the same cancer. I didn't do anything special, I don't think. It's not like he was out smoking ciga-rettes and I had turned vegan.

Here's the thing that's so wrong about what happened. He had so many people who loved him. Devastated parents.

Aunts and uncles. Childhood friends who remembered him. Loved him. And he had Maggie.

If it had been me, it would have been better. And I'm not just saying that. My parents had died years before. That man in a black robe could have shouted out that I'd gone to join them in the sky. I went away to boarding school and barely remember my elementary school friends. No girlfriend. One hundred and twenty-three people attended Adam's funeral. I counted. Nine people would have come to mine, tops. I mean, Maggie and Adam would've come to my funeral, sure, but they would've had each other after it. That's really what should have happened.

I watched Maggie crying in front of the reddish sandy mound of dirt beside the rectangular hole. The sides of the black fabric they laid around the ground flapped in the wind. People trudged to their cars, heads down. Adam's dad wrapped his arm around his mom, and she tucked into his side as if she couldn't stand on her own.

All the men wore suits. Adam's dad had a black suit with pinstripes. God, twelve years gone, and I still remember so many minute details. The blue sky, wispy clouds. Green, freshly mown, pungent grass.

What I remember most of all, though, from that day is how broken Maggie was. And how wrong it all was. It should have been me.

Maggie. Completely broken. Crushed. Devastated. I stood there, long after everyone else drove away. Without a fucking clue as to what I should say or do. Her slender shoulders shook as she cried.

I couldn't fix it. Change anything. Bring him back. When she was ready, I drove her back to the hotel. That was all I could do.

twelve

Maggie

I clasp my Be Happy flowered file folder while tapping lightly on the doorframe of my boss's office. Jane leads the marketing team. I've worked with her for almost four years now. Her love and passion are fundraising events and advertising, and since my primary responsibility is completing grant forms, she more or less lets me run my own show. While I try to stay out of her hair, every now and then, I need her help. She lifts her head at the noise of my tap. Her perfectly coiffed black bob barely moves. She peers over her spectacles and welcomes me in as she folds the lid to her laptop closed.

"Hi there. How's the Prospect grant application coming?" It's the first time we've applied for this specific research grant, and it's due in less than a month.

"Good," I answer as I sit down in the mid-century modern, wooden chair across from her desk. "They want some of the data on the first three quarters of this year. Our published data is only from last year. The quarterly financial reports from this year are missing some of the information I need. Here's a list of some of what I can't locate."

I lean across the desk to give her the typed-up sheet of questions that Jason provided. She slides her spectacles back up her nose and reads through it then sets it down on her desk.

"I'll ask Stephen. I assume you need it as soon as possible?" She pauses from writing a note on the paper to glance at me.

"Yes. I can meet with him if you prefer."

Stephen functions as our CFO, but he's also on the board. He doesn't actually work in our offices, as he's more of a volunteer on an executive level. He's best friends with Senator McLoughlin, who started The McLoughlin Charity shortly after winning his first congressional seat. I don't expect Jane to put me in direct contact with Stephen, given his bigwig status, but like a good employee, I offer.

She waves her hand at me, dismissing the idea. "I'll get the info for you. Is there anything else?"

I tell her no and pull the door closed on my way out.

When I return to my office, I pick up my phone and call Jason. He answers within two rings.

"I'm getting those answers for you."

"Good. For each of my questions?"

"Yeeessss. Are you joining us for dinner tonight?"

There's a pause before he responds, "Who all is coming?"

"I don't know. I didn't ask." My thumb pounds on the back of my pen to release my frustration. This is his crew, not mine. Sam Duke is his childhood friend. He's close with all the Dukes. I've spent many holiday vacations with the

Duke family, and think the world of them, but Sam's his surrogate brother, and these are his people.

"Do you think it's a large group?"

"Ah, well, I invited Yara. But Janet texted me to ask how many people we were bringing, meaning you and me. It sounded like she was making reservations for a group."

"Janet's coordinating tonight? Why didn't she reach out to me?" He sounds whiny, like an unhappy boy. He cracks me up.

"I don't know. She probably figured she knows us well enough to know I'd be the one inviting others, and you would never invite anyone."

"I don't like groups. And I've had a shit day at work."

"What happened?"

"Dean Schlosberger wants to schedule a meeting. I don't think I did well in the student and peer reviews."

"I'm sure you did fine. You're a great teacher. Everyone likes you."

Jason exhales loudly, and it sounds like a wind tunnel through the phone. "I'll stop by your office to meet you beforehand. We can head over together. Good?"

Before heading out for the evening, I stop in the restroom to freshen up. I'm wearing a dark blue dress with a thick brown leather belt at the waist and my heeled tall brown leather boots. The boots and belt closely match my leather tote. The matching leather is all by chance, but it works to make the outfit pull together. When living on a shoestring budget, it's the little things.

I remove the light brown sweater cardigan I've been wearing all day in our chilly office and release my hair from its ponytail. This morning, I took the time for hot rollers, and some of the bounce survived. After throwing my head upside down to give the hair some body, and swiping on some lip gloss and a little blush, I decide it's as good as it's gonna get and go out to the sidewalk to wait for Jason.

The sidewalk is crowded with folks leaving work and heading home. Some of the folks passing by have phones pressed to their ears. Others hustle down the sidewalk, head down, speaking as if talking to an imaginary friend. It's the earbud movement. Now that wireless earbuds fit so easily into the ear canal, I've noticed it more and more on the city streets. It's not for me. I'd prefer for passersby to see I'm talking into a phone, and that I'm not crazy Sally talking to myself. A little girl weaving down the street with a massive lollypop turns quickly, and her hair flies into the big multi-colored sticky candy. Her lips turn down, and the woman with her bends to her level. I can't hear what she's saying to the little girl, but she doesn't seem pleased.

I do love people watching. I can sit on a bench and watch people pass by and imagine whole lives for each person. My favorite is the couples holding hands. Wondering how they met, how long they've known each other…if they have kids.

Strong arms wrap around my waist from behind, lift my feet off the concrete, and twirl me around in a half-circle. He came up behind me to surprise me, and he succeeded. I clutch at my chest, because if a stranger wraps his arms around you out of the blue it's more than a little frightening. He laughs, pleased he "got me," then intertwines his fingers through mine. We have a fairly long walk to get to Jacob's Pickles.

"Did you ever find out who's going to be there?"

"Nope. Does it matter?" I don't know why he gets so stressed out about these things.

We meld into the throngs of pedestrians hustling to get

somewhere, separating only when we need to pass slower people. Night has fallen over the city, but lights pour out from all different directions. My chest squeezes tight, and my body's reaction to his innocuous comment annoys me.

When we arrive at Jacob's Pickles, I look straight to the bar. Before I can make my way to the long, crowded, wooden oasis, Jason is tugging my hand and leading me to the back of the restaurant. Sam and Ollie Duke both stand as we approach. For years, Jason spent his summers and holidays at Sam and Ollie's parents' ranch in Texas. Ollie still lives in Texas, but he visits his brother every month or two.

The two Texans are essentially family to Jason, but they both bypass Jason to welcome me with a hug. I've come to know them well over the years. They both introduce me to Jackson and his girlfriend, Anna, and to one of their friends, Chase. I explain my roommate, Yara, will be joining us, but she's running late. All the chairs are accounted for, so I conclude this is the entire group. Jason can handle this.

"So, how are ya'll doin'?" Ollie shouts above the restaurant noise. Jason rests his arm behind my chair and looks to me, as he always does, to answer. He's such an introvert. If it's a small group, like me, Sam, and him, he'll actively participate in the conversation. In a big group like this, forget about it. He's going to be silent unless someone draws him into a one-on-one conversation. But he'll listen to everything. After we leave, there won't be anything that was said that he's not aware of.

Anna sits to my right, and she and I are getting to know one another while Jason reads the menu as if it's a riveting suspense novel. The waiter stops by for the drink order, and I order a Bloody Mary. Jason adds, "We'll both have the Bloody BLT, but she doesn't want the egg."

The waiter moves on down the table, and Jason dips down, his mouth close enough to my ear that I feel the warmth of his breath. My muscles tense, and I lean into him, tucked in to his side. "Do you want to split?"

"Sure. What are you thinking?" Unlike Jason, I haven't been studying the menu, but we often split meals, especially in places like this where the portions are enormous and loaded with fat and grease.

"Either the hot chicken biscuit or the chicken, bacon, egg, and cheese. Without the egg, if you don't want it." He angles his menu so I can read the description. This place specializes in fried chicken biscuits, and there's something about the hot sauce that's calling to me. I point at that, and he nods confirmation.

Anna reaches across the table and taps Jackson to pull him out of his conversation with Sam and Ollie. "They're splitting. Do you want to split too?"

Right at that moment, the waiter delivers a platter of an extensive variety of pickles to the table, sliced pickled okra, and deviled eggs.

Jackson sets his beer down and picks up the small plates to spread around the table and tells her, "Yeah, we can share."

Ollie jabs Sam's shoulder. "You're tough out of luck on the sharing, dude. I'm eating a full order. This is my kinda place. Shoulda brought your own *senorita*."

Jason withdraws his arm from behind my chair and rests his elbows on the table. Yara comes bounding in, out of breath, loudly apologizing for being late. She takes the empty seat across from Chase at the end of the table. Every now and then I peer down to their end of the table, curious as to how she's doing, since she and Chase don't know each other. The conversation seems to be flowing, so I assume she's doing fine. It's possible he's flirting with her, which is amusing, given he doesn't have the anatomy she prefers.

Dinner arrives, and Jason artfully cuts the biscuit in half and places his half onto a small appetizer plate, giving me the entree plate and all of the cheese grits. At my insistence that he try them, he leans over and plunges his fork into the melted cheesy goodness. He tastes a small amount, then goes back for a fork full. After swallowing, he licks his lips and nods his approval. From that point on, our forks are in a competition to clean out the bowl first.

During dinner, I learn that Anna knew both Jackson and Chase back at Chapel Hill when she was in undergraduate school and they were roommates in grad school. Jackson is now a lawyer, and he works with Sam. Anna tells me Sam and Jackson are becoming good friends. Anna also shares that she's excited because her old roommate has recently moved back to the States. She's going to be in the MBA program and is at some orientation program tonight. I tap Jason on his arm.

"Anna's old roommate is going to be a student at Columbia. Do you think you'll teach her?"

"Doubtful."

"Don't you teach in the business school?"

"Some."

"You should meet up with Olivia. Help her get oriented." He rolls his eyes. Literally rolls his eyes, as if what I am suggesting is ludicrous. I open my mouth in mock outrage, and Anna just laughs.

"It's okay. I'm sure Olivia has it under control. She moved to Europe on her own and rocked it. She's a superstar. Business school will be a no-brainer for her."

After we've all finished our meals and ordered another

round of drinks, Jason gets up to go to the restroom. Anna leans over and asks, "So, how long have you two been together?"

"Huh? Oh, we're not together. We're just friends."

Her brows come together, and she turns her whole body so she's facing me. "Really? You two act like an old couple."

Sam chuckles. "It's only a matter of time." He points a finger at Ollie and says, "We've got bets."

"Dude, you lost your bet. Your bet was within five years of us meeting her. And we met her their junior year at Dartmouth."

I'm a little confused. "Within five years, what?"

"Within five years you guys would be together. I didn't put a time cap. And, dude, wasn't that a hundred dollar bet?"

Jason returns as Sam grumbles and pulls out a crisp bill for his brother. Ollie's laughing, then leaning over to explain to Yara and Chase what just happened, gloating over his win. Jason's standing behind me, and I look up in time to catch him scowling. He leans down and picks up his empty drink.

"I'm gonna get a beer. You guys want anything?"

Sam pipes up. "Waiter will be back in a minute."

I miss Jason's response, but Sam smirks at whatever facial cue Jason gave him. He doesn't say much, but those of us who know him well can read him. After he leaves, Sam turns to Ollie.

"Double or nothing. Within two years."

Ollie raises his eyebrow and grins at me. "This man is the worst loser. He'll keep betting until he loses his shirt."

Ollie flashes his crisp new hundred-dollar bill in the air and shouts across the restaurant to Jason, "Dude, you owe Sam a hundred!" Jason turns his back to our rowdy table.

If they weren't sitting there betting over whether Jason

and I will end up together, I'd laugh and play along. As it is, I'd rather not continue listening to them negotiate time frames and over-under, so I purposefully shift in my chair and focus on Anna.

Anna is telling me about an upcoming work trip she's taking to South Africa for *National Geographic* when she pauses mid-story and stares at the bar. I follow her gaze and see Jason sitting on a stool beside a woman with long dark hair. Under the dimmed golden lights, her hair reminds me of a dark port wine. She's laughing at something he's said, and I can't look away. Jason doesn't ever socialize like that. He's not the kind of guy other women laugh with. His back is to me, but his head is bowed down, in what must be a deep or at least captivating conversation.

The next thing I know, Yara's standing behind me, blocking my view. She taps my shoulder. "Hey, you ready to head home?"

"Yeah, but we need to pay." I swallow, trying to ignore the sinking sensation in my stomach and the numbness spreading across my cheeks and the tips of my fingers.

"Nah. Sam already picked up the bill for the entire table. We'll have to make sure we cover him next time." Sam almost always insists on picking up the entire bill. He's the founder of a financial services company that went public, and he's done well. Losing a hundred dollars to his baby brother tonight didn't affect him in the least.

After we make our goodbyes, Yara guides me out of the restaurant. I don't interrupt Jason at the bar. He'll see I'm gone.

As soon as we make a left turn out of the restaurant, Yara has her arm around my waist and she pulls me to her side.

"You okay?"

"Yeah. Of course. Why wouldn't I be?"

"Mags," she says in a deep, scolding tone that communicates *drop the bullshit, this is me.*

The night air is chilly, and my nose is dripping from the change in temperature. I inhale deeply through my mouth and exhale.

"Yeah. It's good. It's all good." Then I pull away from her and push down the pavement. "So, tell me about Chase. I couldn't hear your end of the table, but you were cracking up."

She slaps her hand over her forehead and laughs out loud. "Oh, my god. What a player," she exclaims loudly enough that a guy walking the opposite direction glances our way.

"Hitting on you?" She waves her hand in the air to indicate maybe. "What did he do?"

She laughs again, and we continue back to our apartment, arm in arm. She's had a bit to drink and is fully enamored, recapping the night from her end of the table, and I do my absolute best to hear her.

thirteen

Jason

The New Year Without Adam

Adam passed away in the fall, before the holidays. Maggie and I were both in the same mental space that semester. Not in the mood for loud, smoky frat parties. Too young to frequent bars. We were both in our own kind of funk.

Thanksgiving and Christmas, we both went home to our individual families. Well, I went to Texas. She went back to her family in Iowa. But, as normal, the Dukes went on a ski vacation. I invited Mags, and she came out after Christmas and joined all of us.

At that point in time, the Dukes were treating me with kid gloves. They knew I'd had a friend pass away. But they also were with me all summer during my treatments. Knew I had a suppressed immune system.

Every single time Patti passed me, she'd try to swipe her hand over my forehead to covertly check my temperature. Patti didn't try to take over my mom's role, but she couldn't help doing things like that. She was so much a mom.

That year, it was funny. Patti knew I'd invited a friend, and that it was a girl. And, you know, it was my second year in college, and she and Sam Senior were fully aware I was on my own. Independent, even though I was a college kid. But Patti, to use Ollie's words, well, she was a stickler for rules. She led me to one of the unused bedrooms in the ski house they'd rented.

"This will be for your guest." She locked eyes with me, then guided me down the hall and down the stairs, to another bedroom that was essentially a bunk room. "This is where you and the boys will stay." She smiled sweetly then added a stern, "Understand?"

Of course, I told them all she was just a friend. It didn't matter how many times I told them. It was like they didn't believe it. Wouldn't accept it.

The thing was, losing Adam crushed Maggie. She wasn't remotely open to a relationship. No one young should ever die a tragic death. It's the worst kind of bullshit. In addition to the loss and pain, it shocked you. Recalibrated your sense of the universe with a faulty world order.

When I picked Maggie up from the Denver airport, it felt like the one person in the world who understood how I was feeling had finally joined me. It wasn't that the Dukes weren't great. They were. And they were the closest thing to family I had. I mean, they'd tell you I was family. And they are my family. I'm not saying they aren't or trying to undercut how important they are to me. But Maggie, when I picked her up at the airport that day, it was like I could breathe again. That's odd, right? That a friend could have a physical impact?

But that was what we were to each other. When everybody else wanted to crowd in on a deck for apres ski, Mags and I would head back. Remove those heavy ski boots, relax in long underwear, and fix ourselves hot chocolate with a small amount of whiskey and heavy on whipped cream. We'd go into the downstairs den, grab a blanket, and cuddle on the leather chesterfield, watching whatever movie or TV show happened to be playing. It didn't matter. Neither of us felt like talking much, and it was comforting to just be.

For New Year's Eve, the Dukes had reservations at The Little Nell. It wasn't like we'd absolutely have to get dressed up. When skiing, you can get away with casual. But neither Maggie nor I were up for it. The Dukes didn't press and seemed to understand. They told us if we stood out on the balcony, we could probably see the fireworks.

That night was the first time Maggie and I kissed. It was before midnight. We'd watched the fireworks, but they went off way earlier. No, we were sitting on the sofa. Watching Times Square.

I don't think I'll ever forget it. What her soft lips felt like. There were no fireworks, but I could swear I heard them going off. Endless explosions. That first kiss, our first kiss. It was tender. Perfect. A perfect kiss to transition from the old into the new. A perfect kiss between friends. Best friends.

fourteen

Maggie

The rain pounds on my bedroom window, and I stretch in my warm bed. The dark sky fits my mood. I shift my pillows, creating a tall stack to lean on, with the decorative blanket from the end of the bed pulled up around me for an extra layer of warmth. My plan for the day is to hunker down in bed, doing as little as possible, on this rainy Sunday morning.

I scroll through text messages as I deliberate leaving my warm cocoon for coffee. It would be so nice if I had a Keurig machine sitting by my bedside. It's not like I have a long walk to the kitchen. The rental listing for my apartment described it as "cozy," and every New Yorker knows that's a euphemism for closet-sized. It's just the getting out of bed bit that's holding me back from my morning happiness.

My thumb hovers over Jason's messages from last night. *You home?* Sent at 11:02 p.m. He didn't go home with her, then. Thank god. That's what that means, right? What if he texted me, and then went home with her anyway? No, no, his next text, asking about Sunday plans, is at 12:16 a.m., so he definitely didn't sleep with her. Wait, what if he slept with her between those two texts? My heart hammers through my chest, and frustration rises because I am such a ridiculous fool. This is absurd. He's going to do what he wants to do. No matter what happened last night, between him and the woman at the bar, I'm still his best friend. I refuse to cry and instead pull the blanket up around me for comfort.

My finger hovers over the keypad, debating a response, as a knock sounds on my bedroom door.

"Come in." I shove the phone under a pillow, hiding it from Yara. I know she must be checking on me, and I'd rather her not figure out I'm rereading short texts that say nothing.

The door opens at the same time lightning flashes, catching my attention. Seconds later, Jason fills the doorway with water droplets running down his weathered, dark brown Barbour jacket. He shakes his head like a wet dog, and a few drops of water spin into the air. He's holding two venti coffees, plus a white paper bag that has dark spots in places from the rain. He holds out one coffee.

"Thought you might not want to go out for coffee this morning."

Did you sleep with that woman last night? It's on the tip of my tongue, but I bite the words back. My hand feels clammy, and I wipe it on my comforter before reaching out to welcome the coffee.

Jason's thoughtful. He knows me. Not many people have a friend who would bring them coffee in bed. He's the holder of my extra apartment key and my emergency contact.

He comes around all the time. But in this case, I know

him well enough to know my nonresponse to his texts is the real reason he's here. No response isn't my norm. He's checking on me to see if I'm okay. It's our funky little dance. I know he sometimes dates other women, but we don't talk about it. I also know I shouldn't be hurt when he does. I'll go silent and withdraw. He becomes more attentive. Then we find our way back to normal.

He delivers the coffees to my bedside table and hangs his coat on the back of my desk chair. Kicks off his sneakers, grabs his coffee, and climbs into bed on the empty side beneath the covers. As he adjusts the pillows so he can lean back against my headboard, I sip my coffee. My phone now lies uncovered on the bed, but it's gone dark, so he can't see that I was staring at his texts.

"So, how was last night?" I ask.

His socked feet find mine beneath the comforter, and he shifts a little closer to me, so our lower legs are aligned. As he's shifting around to get comfortable, he answers, "Fine. You left without saying goodbye."

I stare out the window and observe the rivulets running down the glass. "It's a nasty storm. I can't believe you came over without an umbrella."

He moves even closer, so our bodies touch, and wraps his left arm around my shoulder, pulling me against his chest. He kisses the top of my head. I haven't brushed my teeth yet. There's no need to check. It's got to be foul, so I try to put distance between us, but he holds me in place.

"Hey, Mags." He lifts my chin so I'm forced to look at him, and I press my lips into a firm line. His brow wrinkles as his thumb strokes my cheek. "Is everything okay?"

I push off and jump out of bed, careful to keep my mouth closed until I'm far enough away he won't smell my putrid breath. I mumble as I head out of my bedroom that yes, everything is fine.

After brushing my teeth, I return. He's still propped back on the pillows, sipping his coffee while holding my phone. I climb back in bed and see he's unlocked the screen. Of course he has. He and I have the same passcode for our phones. We did that years ago so if there was ever an emergency we could get into each other's devices. He's reading a CNN article. An alert probably came through and he tapped it.

He avoids making eye contact as he says, "You didn't answer my texts last night."

"I had already gone to bed. I was about to respond when you knocked on my door."

Still reading the article, he says, "So, everything's okay?"

I nod, but he's not looking at me, so I add a verbal, "Yes."

He tosses the phone down and extends his arms. I fall into his open arms, and he pulls the comforter around us. My sister keeps telling me this relationship with Jason isn't healthy. For years, I've told her she's wrong, but given it feels like we had a fight and this cuddling thing we have going is our make-up routine, her points are starting to coalesce. If I had a boyfriend, what on Earth would he think of my friendship with Jason?

I shut off my mind and press against Jason, resting my head on his chest. The pattern of his heartbeat soothes my frayed emotions. He is my balm. My best friend in the world, and this feeling of peace, an inner warmth that simmers when he's near, it's like no other sensation. The rain outside patters away, but in my room, right here, is bliss. As long as I can shut out any thought of him and the girl from last night. Shut off the nagging idea that I shouldn't care.

I exhale and stretch, leaning my head far to the side to stretch my always so tight shoulder muscles. Jason kneads my shoulder one-handed. "You are tight." He moves both of our coffees and sets them on the side table. Then he aligns his back with the headboard again and positions me between his legs, my back to him. With a firm grip, he squeezes my tight, tense shoulder muscles, then releases and kneads my upper back and up along my neck. His strong fingers twist through my mass of hair and massage the base of my scalp.

It's been years since I had a massage, or anyone touched me like this, working my muscles and releasing tension. Outside, rain patters against the window, but in my room, right now, is heaven. My head drops like a rag doll's, and a moan escapes.

His hands abruptly drop to my sides, and he squeezes my hip. I lift my head and plead, "Don't stop."

He pulls at the base of my t-shirt. "Take this off and lie down."

I lift the pajama top and hesitate midway as the cool air touches my exposed belly and the underside of my breasts. He caresses my bare waist gingerly as if I am fragile or valuable.

"It's okay. I've seen it all, remember?"

My cheeks burn, and my heartbeat races higher on a sprint, sprung out of the blissful, restful state from seconds ago. He gently pushes me forward, silently instructing me to lie face down.

I exhale and pull the shirt off over my head, my back to Jason, and lie down flat on the bed, over the top of the comforter. Jason grabs onto my flannel pajama pants. "These too. I'm going to pull them down. Your muscles are tight. You need a massage."

He's correct. I do. I believe in the therapeutic benefits of massage; it's just I haven't prioritized massages in my financial budget. Or in my calendar either. I didn't mean for so much time to go by without taking care of myself.

Cool air tingles against my skin as he lowers my flannel bottoms. For a moment, I'm laid bare to him, in only my black cotton panties. He's silent and still. The dip in the mattress on one end shows he's still on the bed, but I rise on my elbow to see him. His eyes are dark, and he breathes in and out of his mouth.

"Are you—"

He straddles me, the sudden movement halting my words as he covers my back with his strong hands, stroking up and down. He pushes me flat onto the bed, and I turn my head to the side so I can breathe. For minutes, he rubs my back, up and down, kneading the muscles, manipulating knots and forcing release. *Magical. Glorious. Heavenly.* These are the words that are floating through my mind as I relax into his touch. I won't overthink this. I will enjoy this. No, I will revel in this.

He shifts farther back, off my rump and onto the back of my thighs. I brace myself, expecting his hands to return to my body, wondering where they'll land, what he'll touch. I have had masseuses manipulate the muscles in my ass, and it's a combination of peculiar and restorative. The buttock muscles are strong muscles that tie into major muscle groups. Intellectually, I recognize it's good for the body. However, the movement feels intimate, and imagining Jason's hands touching my private areas has me tensing in anticipation.

He positions his body over mine, straddling me, radiating

heat mere inches above me. Goosebumps rise all over my exposed flesh.

"Do you have massage oil?"

I involuntarily clench my thighs together in reaction to his deep timbre.

"I don't."

He shifts back onto my thighs. The cold air and his pulling back sounds off an internal alarm because the last thing I want is for this to end.

"I have baby oil."

He hops off me and pads barefoot into my bathroom. Cool air wraps around me. I stretch my arms above my head. My body flattens to the bed, and my breasts spill out from the sides. Jason comes to stand by the bed, and I roll onto my side to better see him. His gaze sears. It's a hard, heated gaze, one he rarely makes. I roll farther onto my side, giving him a more complete view of my bare breast. My breath catches, but I do not look away. My panties are damp, and I shift my hips, squeezing the muscles to coax my sex. He focuses on the subtle movement. In silence, I dare him to touch me. Not as a friend, but as a lover.

He grips the bottom of his t-shirt, raises it over his head, and throws it to the floor. I watch his nimble fingers unbutton his jeans, and they drop to the floor. He's wearing cotton boxers, but from the tented shape, I know he's affected, and it's not in a friend zone kind of way. He's turned on.

He climbs back on the bed and resumes his position, straddling me over my thighs. A warm liquid drips down my spine. The mattress shifts from his weight as he leans to place the baby oil bottle at the end of the bed. Then he spreads the silky oil on my back in smooth strokes, up and down, caressing the curves of my waist, across my shoulders. His oily hands slip between my body and the sheet, and he cups my breasts, spreading the oil while tweaking my sensitized nipples. I gasp, and he pauses. Fear that he's going to stop, that my noise made him aware of what he's doing courses through me. He does not notice. He firmly grasps my breasts, kneading the hypersensitive skin, and I can't hold back a louder moan of pleasure. As he leans over me, his hard erection presses along my ass. I lift my upper body slightly to give him greater access. His fingers circle my nipples and pinch. I close my eyes, luxuriating in the sensation. The knife's edge of pain and pleasure.

I rotate onto my back, baring myself completely to him, and he lowers his body, covering my lips with his. When he kisses me, it's gentle at first. Soft, tender, and slow. And as I open for him, and our tongues tease and explore, a surreal sensation falls over me. None of this feels real. The rain outside composes a soothing backdrop for this erotic massage playing out in my bed on a slow Sunday morning.

Then the slowness intensifies as Jason repositions himself between my legs, his hard cock pressing against the apex of my thighs, and an urgency arises as his hips thrust against me. I reach down, sliding my hand below the waistband of his boxers, and find his silky tip. My thumb smooths the bead of moisture, then I grip his cock and squeeze while sliding my hand up and down. He groans as I pick up the pace, applying strong pressure. His eyelids half close, his expression one of ecstasy. I move to slide down his body, to take him in my mouth, but he stops me.

He reaches over for the baby oil and applies pressure to

my shoulder to force me to lie on the bed, then drips oil from the center of my breasts to the top of my panties. He spreads the oil along my belly, my waist, and arms, but he spends extra time with my breasts, kneading and caressing and dropping to take my nipple in his mouth, using his tongue to caress them into peaks.

I'm on the verge of begging as the need to have him climbs, and I whimper. With a trail of baby soft, tender kisses, he works his way down. He drags my drenched panties down my legs then nips and kisses his way back up my thigh, situating himself between my legs. I rise up on my elbows so I can watch. I want to see. I don't want to ever forget this. My thigh muscles quiver. I'm sensitized, reactive to the softest touch, but he doesn't seem to mind as his tongue travels up and down, working me, until he homes in on my most sensitive area. His mouth clamps down on my clit, and I shriek as my first orgasm rolls through me. My toes curl in, the sensation forcing my eyes closed, sending me spiraling. I gasp from pleasure, for air, as my core quivers.

When I open my eyes, he's between my legs and easing into me, and all I can repeat is, "Yes. Yes. Yes," over and over, barely coherent, as he thrusts up and takes me the way I've wanted him and needed him. We move in unison, gasping at times as he hits the very best spot deep within me. He angles my knee upward and drives forward, pounding over and over, and I swear he slams against my cervix. I look to the side of the room as emotion rocks through me, and he grunts, "Look at me."

I do, and those soulful eyes sear me. I love this man. With every ounce of my being. He is my everything, and I would do anything for him. Give him anything.

"Mags. Love you. So much." The intensity of the moment pushes me over, and I quiver. His movements become erratic as he penetrates deep within, and another orgasm rolls through me, my muscles clenching and coaxing him as his facial muscles contract. He arches as he moans, loses control, and releases into me. I feel him, deep inside me, contracting, filling me. His expression is one of pure rapture. He falls onto me, his back damp from exertion. I rub his back, exploring the contours and loving my newfound freedom to do so.

There's a quick tap at the door, and I hear it open. Yara's voice fills the room. "Hey, you wanna—" Then there's a quick pause and the door slams shut. I press my mouth to Jason's shoulder as I giggle, imagining what she just saw. Jason's bare ass lying between my spread legs, both of us completely naked.

Jason pulls away from me and sits on the end of the bed. He slaps my thigh and pops a loud kiss on my forehead then jumps off the bed and lumbers around searching for his clothes.

I roll to my side to watch him. He tosses my clothes my way when he finds them. Except for my panties. He leaves those on the floor. He walks to my dresser and opens my panty drawer, because yes, he knows where I keep them. He's been in here more than once while I put away laundry. He pulls out a white pair and sends them sailing through the air to me.

"You might need a fresh pair."

I still haven't moved from the bed. It's Sunday, and my personal preference would be for us to stay here. Maybe order lunch in.

He rubs his hand in rapid-fire succession on his scalp, back and forth, as if he's aiming to make the hairs stick up. I watch him while I lie naked in the bed. He rests his arm against the window, staring out at the dark, gray sky. "Get dressed. Let's go grab lunch."

I glance at the clock. It's not even 10:30. I exhale slowly, counting to ten in my head. He raps the window with his knuckle, facing the rain. "Get dressed."

My face heats as I sit up, unease stirring in my belly. I pull on the white panties, my flannel bottoms, and then my top. He remains fixated on something outside, his back to me.

I step up to him and stroke his back. He exhales and turns to face me, his movement forcing me to let go. "I forgot. I'm supposed to meet Sam this afternoon. I should probably head down to his place." His head is shaking back and forth like a bobble doll. I've never seen anything like it. Right before he reaches my door, he turns back to me.

"We didn't use a condom again. Shit."

My lungs contract, and for a moment it's like they aren't working, like they stopped taking in air. "I'll go on the pill."

"Okay, good." With his hand on the doorknob, his back to me, and his head angled down to the floor, he adds, "If I'm with anyone else, I'll be sure to use a condom," he mutters.

Anyone else.

He said it like an afterthought, reassuring himself. When the door closes behind him, I slump on the floor.

Anyone else.

At some point later, the door opens. "It's about—"

Once again, Yara doesn't finish her sentence. She stoops beside me and pulls me into her arms. She doesn't ask questions. She simply repeats things along the lines of him being an asshole. He doesn't deserve my friendship. She goes on and on saying things to make me feel better, and I let her. I let her hold me as shock waffles through my core.

I never would have expected that...not from him. Friends, who fuck? That's what he wants?

That's what he wants.

fifteen

. . .

Jason

The Day It Returned

When I moved to New York, it was for grad school. I did my master's and doctorate at Columbia. Before we moved, our senior year, applications to grad school, interviews, campus visits, making plans for the move, all of it consumed most of my time.

My cancer had been in remission. We weren't using the acronym NED, meaning no evidence of disease, but it was a thing of the past. Kind of. I mean, I had a scar. A daily reminder of my past. Little things worried me. Fevers. If I didn't feel good. If my glands felt swollen. Nausea.

I figured I'd find a new doctor when I got settled in New York. I was a little late on my check-up and scan that year. Nothing to be too concerned about. I felt fine. Energized.

Maggie took a job in New York too. She found an apartment near mine. She sold her Honda before moving, so we rode together from New Hampshire to New York. It felt pretty exciting that day, driving down. My Jeep packed to the gills, so crammed with stuff I couldn't see out the rearview mirror. We blared the music, windows down.

I didn't tell Maggie when I got around to going in for my scan. It was supposed to be a simple check-up. When I got the call to come in to discuss my results, just from her tone, before the nurse finished her first sentence, I knew.

I had decided I was going to keep it from Maggie. She'd lost Adam. Had been devastated. She'd be worried about me. We'd just moved to Manhattan. We were twenty-two. She had other things to be doing with her time. New friends to make. New career.

I had some papers from the doctor on my kitchen counter. Some papers I needed to go through. Insurance. It could be such a pain in the ass.

Anyway, she saw the papers. I stood there, watching her read them. I should've been pissed that she picked them up. I had every right to decide who to tell. Who to bring into it. But she looked so sad, standing there processing my results. And it hurt me. Like my chest was being ripped open and pummeled. I never ever wanted to hurt her. In any way.

And you know, that's the thing. A life with me, every fucking year that goes by, life can get flipped upside down. It could come back. Any day. My plans are meaningless. Can't count on anything. That's not the life I want for her. Not then. Not now. Not ever.

sixteen

Maggie

"So, what do you think?" Yara asks, poking the corner of the menu into my bicep so hard it'll probably bruise.

"Ow! It's cool." It's a Tuesday night, and Yara has forced me off the sofa. We're at Helen's, a rather novel downtown restaurant she's been wanting to come to for ages. I'm drawn to the brick-vaulted ceilings, but the East Asian design elements are what set this place apart.

I scan the menu, and it's clear the East Asian influence extends to the cocktail menu as well. I'm drawn to the Lost in Tokyo drink, but it includes prune juice, and that's a no. Prune juice reminds me of my grandmother's home remedies. I ultimately choose the lychee martini after confirming with our waitress it's not too sweet, and Yara chooses a drink with tapioca pearls mixed in.

Yara picks up her phone to continue a text conversation she's having with a colleague. They have a business partner who is being a tad secretive about an upcoming meeting, and they've converted into conspiracy theorists, debating all the possible interpretations of the woman's behavior. More than once, I've been thankful I didn't choose corporate America after being subjected to Yara's detailed analysis of inner company political workings. And at this moment, I'm filled with gratitude that Yara has her colleague to dissect today's events with, and therefore I don't have to sit there and constantly ask questions like, "And who is Jim again?"

While she taps away on her cell, at times looping me in with an update like, "Ronnie says there's a possibility they may be looking to sell the division," I read the menu. I learn that the focal point of the restaurant, a lotus wall panel, represents the wheel of life, the law of cause and effect, and reincarnation. I also learn that a lotus represents purity, rooted in mud, and growing toward the light. Something that could apply to each of us, I suppose.

The teakwood paneling lining the sides of the restaurant depicts the deepest forest, where few humans ever go. I am sure they are referencing some sort of spiritual quest, but I can't help but wonder if maybe that deep forest lies within. A forest so thick we build walls to avoid risking losing ourselves in the nebulous depths. Our fear so great of what might consume us, we are afraid to tread in the unlit unknown. And yes, of course, I'm thinking of Jason. I know in my heart of hearts he loves me. Sunday proved he does, in fact, or at least can, find me sexually attractive. Yet, for the second time, he closed down. Built a wall. Shut me out.

I'm sipping my white martini, perusing a Cambodian temple sculpture, when Yara's hand over mine draws me out of my spiraling rumination. A twisted range of emotion has been flowing up and down on repeat since Sunday, and I haven't been able to eliminate the disturbance.

She flips her phone over, face down. "Enough. I'm here for you. No more work. Tell me, how'd day two of Jason detox go?"

I haven't responded to any calls or texts since Sunday. That's the main reason I agreed to travel downtown this evening. The probability he will come over tonight is high. He doesn't do well when I don't answer him. My avoidance will only go so far, though. He'll most likely show up at my office tomorrow. And I don't want to lose our friendship. I'll play it off, like what he did didn't hurt me. I just need some time and space before then. I sip my drink without answering her. It feels like a bitchy question.

She sighs and sets about hunting down tapioca pearls with her straw, downing about half her cocktail in the process. Then she slaps her palm on the table, resolute.

"You know, I feel like a woman counseling a friend, and I'm telling her all the time, 'He's never gonna leave her,' and the friend nods and says, 'I know,' and continues seeing the guy. But here's the thing—there is no her. He's just not that into you. I don't know why. But he's not. Maybe it's that you guys fart around each other. You've been hanging out forever. Like that bridge has been crossed, and there's no crossing back to the side with possibilities. You are now firmly entrenched on the other side, and you need to venture forward on your own."

Yara stares at me, expecting a response. She's not wrong. But it hurts, a deep, aching pressure in the middle of my chest. A crushing pain so intense at times it's like I am below water, struggling to surface for air. Her warm hand covers my frigid one. My eyes sting. Warm tears fall, and I swipe them away.

"Shit, sweetie. I don't even know what you see in him. He's boring as fuck. Barely speaks. Sits like a depressed lump."

"Stop it." I pull away from her and place both of my hands below my thighs, to warm them and keep away from her. She can't touch me while saying those things.

"Look, I'm not the one between you guys. If he made you happy, I wouldn't say a word. But you're miserable. And you can do so much better! It's like a Band-Aid. You've got to rip that baby off. Let some oxygen surround that sore so it heals."

"Ewww."

"But you get the point, right? You've got to do something drastic. You said that one day you'd like to return to the Midwest, right?"

"Yeah." When I moved after college, it was never supposed to be forever. I'm a midwestern girl. I'm not saying I want a cornfield in my back yard, but I always thought I'd have a yard, kids, and a dog. I'm not entirely sure how ten years have gone by so quickly and I'm in the same apartment I moved into a decade ago.

"Sweetie, I don't want you to move. But moving will give you space. I might not get this whole thing between you and Jason, but I've observed it for eons. You two spend so much time together you suffocate out any chance for other possibilities. It's like an acorn at the bottom of a forest floor. With no sun, how is it ever going to take root?"

Hmmm, am I currently deep in the forest, where few humans ever go? I focus on a spot on the forest decal, toward the floor, and the pain in my core intensifies.

In a soft voice, she says, "You're thirty-two."

"I'm aware," I grit out. Actually, not quite thirty-two. It's looming. As are my forties.

"Well, shit or get off the pot! No. That doesn't work for you. You were never on the pot. You've gotta get over this guy!"

"But we're sort of sleeping together now, so I am kind of..."

"Which makes it worse!" Her body springs forward forcefully, and a few heads turn our direction. I bow my head.

Unaware she's drawing attention from others, she continues. "He's no closer to treating you as anything more. And what an ass, by the way. I mean, really, if he loves you as a friend, how can he do this to you? Stand up to him. Move on. Go get the life you want."

She pats me on the head and mutters something about loving me, then excuses herself to go to the bathroom. It seems that's the conclusion of my scolding for the night, and now we can transition to dinner. Her heart is in a good place, and I do love her for it, but that doesn't mean I'm ready to hear her.

When she leaves, I dig into my tote bag and locate my cell. Jason didn't call on Monday. He needed space too. He did leave flowers for me at reception. Today, I have six missed calls and three texts from him.

> **Jason**
> Want to grab dinner tonight?

> **Jason**
> Are we okay?

Jason
Call me. Please.

The last text came through within the last hour. He might have already stopped by my apartment and seen I'm not home. My fingers are hovering over the keyboard, debating responding, when Yara returns to the table. She glances down and pulls my phone away.

"Do not even think about it."

I nod. It's the only agreement I can force. But…his texts sound broken. And I know he's got to be emotional. He's got to be worried about our friendship, and I don't want him to worry. I don't want him to doubt if our friendship is safe when it is. He will always have me in his life. No matter what. He can always depend on me. He doesn't have many people in his life, and Yara doesn't understand that. Not only does she have a huge family and a mound of colleagues, she has a whole vibrant world of fellow lesbians who surround her, encourage her, and love her. It's hard for someone with such an enormous support network to comprehend how devastating it could be to someone like Jason, who has such a small caring group in his life.

Our food comes, and we both eat. I don't taste much, but Yara says the food is delicious. I might be coming down with a cold. That could explain my chest pain and my inability to focus. I massage my throat, feeling to see if my glands are swollen. As I do so, a wave of nausea hits me. Jason. This is around the time of year he gets his scan. What if he got his results back, and I didn't answer the phone today?

Everything we have going on between us means nothing if his cancer has returned. And if that's the case, he needs me. Right now, he needs me. I can overlook what happened

Sunday. Everyone has said for years that eventually we'd have sex. That happened, and now we just have to deal with it. Sex is a little thing. If his cancer is back, that's a big thing. He'll need me.

Yara's studying me. She's not going to like it when I don't return home with her. But she'll deal. She's already texting someone she met recently about meeting up for a drink.

I need to know Jason's okay.

seventeen

Jason

The Night We Stayed In

When did it all begin? When did the pain first surface? So much of my twenties blends together, I can't pinpoint a beginning.

I've thought a lot about it. I don't think I would've made it through everything without Maggie. In college, we stayed in when I needed to. When the risk of flu was super high, or if I wasn't feeling great, I didn't have to be alone. She was my friend, always checking in. She got a box of those masks, and if she felt like she might be getting sick, she'd wear one. Make me wear one too. She bought me orange juice. Always read about foods I should be eating. Kale. Good god. She tried to force-feed me so much kale. But she did find some rather delicious smoothie blends.

In college, she picked up the role of caretaker. She's never really stopped. But for years, she made the decisions for us. If she wanted to go out, and I felt well enough, we went out. She made sure we had plenty of social interaction with groups of people. She's an extrovert. It's natural for her.

When we first moved to New York, we still went out together. Sam had recently moved to New York too, and I'd go out with him about once a week. Maggie usually joined us. This was back before his company went public and he made it big. He didn't socialize a lot, but when he did, we'd go to bars. He'd usually meet folks—well, a girl with friends in tow—and we'd end the night in a group. I'd also go out with classmates, and she'd join us. Maggie discovered Team in Training, and sometimes she'd hang with that group, and she'd bring me along. We spent a lot of time together, but she was still more or less the social activities director.

Then our first New Year's Eve in Manhattan arrived. We'd just come back from our annual trip skiing with the Dukes. I was sitting on her sofa, waiting for her. She opened her bedroom door, and wow. That dress. So short. Tight. Sparkly. Super high heels. It's almost ten years later, and I still remember her legs that night. Black hose. Something about the way the light hit the curves.

We were supposed to go to a party with Sam and Ollie. Ollie knew a ton of people, and he always gathered a big group of friends. And I knew. If we went out that night as planned, she'd meet some guy. In that dress and those heels, damn. Hot as hell. There was no way tons of guys wouldn't be hitting on her. Even with me standing beside her, because Ollie would make wisecracks about us just being friends. He'd force out our usual denials. And then every guy there would know she was available.

She wanted to go. She was dressed up on New Year's Eve. Sitting at home with me wasn't what she wanted. But I could see what was going to happen, and it scared me. Terrified me. So, I told her I wasn't feeling well. It probably wasn't the first time I claimed to not feel well to avoid going out, but it was the first time Maggie really wanted to go out that I feigned being sick. I told her she should still go out, at least, I think I did. But she refused, like I supposed I knew she would.

New Year's Eve in New York City. We stayed in that night. We sat in her apartment and watched the ball drop on TV. She kept checking my temperature. Told me not to worry about it, that her feet thanked her for staying in. I don't know if that's exactly when things changed between us. But that night, something shifted.

It became easier to stay in, just the two of us. I suppose one of the reasons that night stands out to me is because that night, it wasn't just that I didn't feel like going out. I was afraid of losing Maggie. And at the same time, I knew I couldn't have Maggie. Here's a little life truth. When you love someone more than life itself, but you can't be with that person, in every single way, it hurts. On a scale of one to ten? Ten.

eighteen

Maggie

Jason lives in a row of identical townhomes on 116th Street. All the town homes have been subdivided into apartments. I step past one of his neighbors who is sitting on the concrete step smoking a cigarette. I don't know her name, but we both recognize each other and smile. She doesn't pay any attention as my key twists in the lock.

When I reach Jason's apartment door, I lightly rap on the heavy wood as I push it open. Jason's sitting on his sofa, and a sporting game plays on the tube. He's not alone. Sam's with him. Two open beers rest on the coffee table.

Sam smiles the moment he sees me and comes around to give me a welcoming hug. "Hey, sweetie. How're things?"

I look at Jason. If Sam's here, does that mean his check-up didn't go well? I step to the front of the coffee table and face him. Jason stands and bends to press a soft kiss to my cheek. When he sits, he pulls me down to sit beside him, squeezed into his corner to give Sam ample room. He rests his hand over mine, and his thumb caresses my knuckles in a slow back and forth. He's touching me in a way that is confusing as hell.

"Things are good. How about with you?" I ask Sam while watching Jason, studying him. I have an urge to yank my hand out of his and get answers. Check his kitchen counter for papers, any kind of sign as to what's going on with him, but I continue my conversation with Sam.

"My mom is hoping you guys will come join us skiing this year. We've got plenty of room." We've gone with Sam's family to his house in Aspen for years. Jason hasn't mentioned it to me this year.

"I'd love to if Jason is up for it." Jason rubs my back, up and down, and in slow circles. The movement is reminiscent of the massage, and I jump up. It's too much. I can't handle it. I came by to see if he's okay. That's what I need to do.

When I land in the chair across from the sofa, Jason gives me a questioning glance but doesn't say anything. He picks up his beer and swallows.

"Did you get your results back?"

"Doctor said all looks good. Results will take a while. Can I get you something to drink?"

"No. I'm good. I just came from dinner." I avoid looking at Jason and tap my foot until the dull thump fills the void. There's a tension between us, but Jason, as always, seems oblivious. "And actually, Sam, Jason may have a different girl to invite skiing this year." I aim for casual and nonchalant as I say it and hope the anger and hurt simmering below the surface remains undetected.

"There's no one else," Jason says, wrinkles forming

around his eyes, the expression he has when he's confused about something.

"The girl from the other night? Just a casual hook-up, then?" I ask.

Jason frowns but doesn't respond. Maybe a little of the venom I'm feeling seeped out.

Sam downs the rest of his beer, glances at his watch, and says, "I'm gonna get out of here. You two take care. Let me know about ski plans."

"I'll head out too. I only stopped by because I—" I don't know how to complete the sentence, so I don't. I gather my pocketbook and slip on my shoes, and Jason's fingers wrap around my bicep. His fingers could wrap around my arm and almost touch. I step to follow Sam out the door, but Jason doesn't let go.

"Stay for a minute."

Sam's out the door without looking back. It's as if he can't get out of the apartment quickly enough. No question where his loyalties lie. I spin on my heels and rip my arm out of his grasp. It's probably the first time I've ever pulled away from Jason, and the action surprises both of us.

"What's wrong?"

"Nothing, Jason. Why would anything be wrong?" I stick out my chin and push my shoulders back. There's a surge of annoyance and anger that strengthens me. We both know exactly what's wrong, so why is he asking?

He shuffles his feet and stuffs his hands into his jean pockets. "Well, stay for a bit. We can find a show."

"No. I was out with a friend, and you asked me to come over. You made it sound important. I'm glad everything is okay. But I'm gonna go out and find Yara and continue our night." In reality, I'll go home and read or watch TV, but he doesn't need to know that. I grip the knob, ready to leave.

"Don't be like this." His tone is soft, pleading.

"Like what, Jason? Like it hurts that you are sleeping with me and other women? That I'm your fallback. That you ask me over so you aren't lonely?"

"I can't lose you." He's staring over my shoulder, and I can't be certain if he's speaking to me or the wall.

I twist the knob, pull the door open, and with one foot out the door, tell him, "You won't lose me. We'll always be friends. But, Jason, you are a recluse. For years, I loved it. It felt like you and I were locked away in our little world. But it's suffocating. You need to figure out why you never want to do anything outside of your den. Why you find it so hard to open up. Because I need to not be so dependent on you. And that's going to mean you can't be so dependent on me."

"You're my best friend. What do you mean? Of course, I'm dependent on you. Mags, please. Tell me what I can do to make things better. I need you in my life. What do you want me to do?"

"Love me, be with me, don't just fuck me like a random…" I take a deep breath and try not to let tears fall. "See a therapist. Talking helps. Go to a therapist. Talk about whatever it is that's going on in your head. About whatever it is that you keep bottled up."

If anything, maybe he'll go see someone who helps him see he's not being fair to me. This friendship zone we're in isn't healthy anymore. Something has to change.

I pull the door behind me and don't look back. I can't. I don't need to, anyway. I know exactly what I would see. His apartment door. And behind that door, I'd bet money he's standing there, staring at the door, with his hands in his pockets.

nineteen

Jason

"Jason, why don't you tell me what's going on?"

The couch Dr. Clemmons has in her office isn't particularly comfortable. I expected the kind you see in the movies, that you can lie down on and stare at the ceiling. This one is more of a bucket seat contraption and it forces you to either sit back or shift forward.

"Jason. What brings you in here?"

I'm not a moron. I do know I need to speak. Unfortunately, they don't make pills that fix everything. I need to speak. Maggie will walk out of my life unless I do this. "I'm not sure where to start."

"Well, why don't we start with you telling me why you decided to schedule the appointment? What prompted that decision?"

"I have a friend who has been trying to get me to come see a therapist for a long time."

Shit, this couch is uncomfortable. I snatch one of her bright, happy throw pillows and shove it behind my back.

Dr. Clemmons offers a soft smile. A notepad sits on her lap, propped up by her crossed legs, and a pen rests in her still hands. She's about my age. Which is fine, I suppose. She comes highly recommended. There's an awkward silence in the room. She decides to do her job and continues asking me questions.

"Why does your friend want you to see a therapist?"

"I don't know."

She angles her head inquisitively but doesn't say anything. No, she wants me to speak.

"They recommended that I see a therapist when I was diagnosed with cancer. And after a close friend passed away." I add the last part to explain. Not everyone with cancer has to see a therapist. Maybe if I'd gone to the support groups, instead of skipping them with Adam, none of my doctors would have thought to push therapy on me.

"Are you currently undergoing treatment?"

"No. No. I'm in remission." She jots something down on her pad. Score one point to me; I said something she wants to remember.

"How long have you been in remission?"

"Almost seven years."

Her eyebrows rise, and she makes another notation. Two points. *Ding, ding.*

"So, you said a friend has wanted you to see a therapist for a long time. Years, it seems. What changed, for you to come here now?"

Seven years later. I get her point. And I don't like these open-ended questions. I prefer mathematical questions. I prefer numbers. She doesn't say anything. Five or ten minutes go by, and she doesn't say anything, and it's clear that she's putting this on me.

"Maggie believes…I don't know what she believes."

"Who is Maggie?"

"She's my friend. My best friend." Her pen moves across the notepad. Three points for Jason.

"And you said Maggie believes…Maggie believes what?"

Maggie never agreed with Adam and me skipping out on our support group. But Adam bore the brunt of that. He told me some of what she said. Probably not everything.

Dr. Clemmons's eyebrows raise. "What would you like to talk about today?"

"I need to show Maggie I'm trying so I don't lose her. You tell me. How do we start?"

Dr. Clemmons makes a notation. Four points.

"Why would you lose her?"

"I think it's becoming difficult for her to be my friend."

"We can all be difficult at times. What makes you think this?"

"I never want to go out. I always want us to stay in."

"Can you tell me more about that?"

This is why I hate therapists. They dig and dig. They keep digging until you are broken down crying.

"Jason, is it difficult for you to talk about what's going on?"

I stare at her straight, shiny, black hair.

"No." She stares back at me. Fuck. "I just don't know what to say."

She gives me a sympathetic smile. Bet she's heard that one before. Come on then, keep digging.

"Well, that's okay. We can just sit here in silence if you want."

That, I wasn't expecting. I blow out frustration, and she smiles, almost amused.

"Jason, some people need the time just to sit and think. Some people need to get it all out in a rush. Some people can't find the words, so they draw pictures or write it down. At the end of the day, I'm here for you, in whatever way you need."

I shrug. I don't know what I need.

"Maybe…" I start to speak but already feel fucking stupid. I don't want to talk. She raises her eyebrows wanting me to continue. "Maybe the writing…I don't know."

"Sure, let's start there." She gets up and retrieves a notebook from a shelf, flips through it, then hands it to me.

We sit in silence as I try to write down my feelings, and I realize this was the wrong idea. I write and scribble it out. Write, scribble, write, scribble. I want to ball it all up and chuck it on the floor, but I don't want to look like a moron. After more minutes tick by, I end up just writing her name.

Maggie.

"Do you think it might be helpful if I give you some questions to answer? As writing prompts? You wouldn't have to answer anything you didn't want to."

I shrug. I can do it if that's what she wants.

She takes the notebook back from me and sits down at her desk and writes away. *Ding ding ding.* Many, many points for Jason.

When I get home, I open my laptop to review my notes on the upcoming journal article that's due soon if I hope to get it published in this academic year. I make essentially no headway. Dean Schlosberger will not be pleased.

twenty

Maggie

"Whatcha doing?" Yara's shrill question forces me to shift the phone away from my ear. Yara has a tendency to be loud. Right now, she's in a bar, which serves to increase her volume.

"Not much. I'll be home soon."

"You're bringing juice by Jason's, aren't you? It's Monday. Juice delivery day."

"For this week. I'll tell him he needs to start buying it himself."

"Uh-huh. I've heard that one before. Well, Jennifer and I are at The Lounge if you want to stop by after you deliver groceries. If you don't get sucked into his sofa." Laughter rings through the phone. Other people near her are laughing at her weak joke. "Love you!"

She can be such a bitch. "Love you too!"

I have absolutely no business bringing juice by Jason's

apartment. But I have for eons. Because I know if I don't do it, he won't go out and buy it. And I don't know how to stop. Because I love him. I ball my hands into tight fists, forcing my nails against my palm to the point of physical discomfort. *How am I supposed to stop caring about him?*

I twist the key in his apartment door. Maybe I'll be lucky, and he won't be home yet. I can drop off the juice in his refrigerator, leave the financial statements he seems obsessed with for him to analyze, and get the hell away. Meet Yara and her new love interest. Observe mutual attraction in play.

"Hey, there you are. I went ahead and ordered from Szechuan Garden." So much for getting in and out. Monday nights, we tend to do Chinese, so of course, he went ahead and ordered. I've been putting space between us, and he hasn't even noticed. Moving on as if we didn't just have the biggest fight of our friendship.

I close the refrigerator door and pull out my updated reports. I have it all on an Excel sheet, but my boss gave me strict instructions not to share it with anyone. Somehow, printing them and sharing them feels less like skirting the line. All I need is for him to help me figure out the percentage raised used for operations and the cost to raise $100. Year to date, or the first two quarters. It's not really that easy to figure out, though. Charitywatch.org rates charities based on this data, only they haven't yet rated The McLoughlin Charity.

"I went to a therapist." He takes the papers from me.

"Really?" My eyebrows rise so high I imagine they might be approaching my hairline.

He holds the papers at his waist, looking like the student I used to know, in his jeans and t-shirt. He's hardly groveling, but the way his shoulders cave forward combined with his dejected expression, I get that he's trying. He's waving the white flag.

"Wow. Good. How did it go?"

He shrugs, his go-to non-committal response. "Do you want something to drink? Beer? Wine?"

With drinks in hand, we make our way to his sofa to await our dinner delivery. As I sink onto the cushion, I remember Yara's comment. I really should get out of here and meet up with Yara. But instead, I tap his wine glass with mine. "So, tell me. The therapist. Was it good?"

"Not much to tell. It was a get-to-know-you session."

"Are you going to see her again?" I hold my breath.

"Yeah. You want me to." He's staring at the carpet. Or maybe the coffee table.

"Jason, you can't go to therapy because I want you to. You've got to go because you want to. Otherwise, you won't get anything out of it."

"I don't want to lose you. If you think I should see a therapist, I'll do it. You're not the first person to suggest it."

I study him, which is easy to do since his gaze is affixed at something far away from me. At least he's going. Maybe the therapist can make some headway. Help him let go of Adam. It's obvious he's never gotten over losing his friend. And he tries to project that on me, always worried I'm still trying to get over him. I loved Adam. I did. But it was thirteen years ago. He was my first love. Unlike Jason, I did see one of Dartmouth's therapists at the counseling center. Sure, there's a part of me that misses Adam. A part that yearns for what could have been. It's painful. A dream so close you can almost touch it, and then it slips away.

In the last ten years, I've raised $175,000 for cancer research, so other people don't lose their loved ones. My nonprofit career centers around fighting cancer, and The McLoughlin Charity has raised tens of millions for research. I've found ways to cope. I am strong.

Jason doesn't sleep well. My friends think he's depressing. I believe he's hurting. Still.

After we eat, Jason smiles. "You're gonna love this. Tonight, *The Notebook* is playing."

"You hate that movie."

"Hate is a strong word. But you like it." He reaches for my socked foot, pressing right along the ball of my foot. "So, we'll watch it."

Holy cow. It's the little things. The little things Yara doesn't understand about Jason and me. His foot massages are out of this world, probably better than sex. There are husbands out there who don't treat their wives as well as Jason treats me.

He's right in that I do love this movie. I get teary-eyed every time it comes on, at least if I manage to watch the ending. But if he wanted to watch Chicago PD or CSI, I'd be fine with it.

I refill both our wine glasses and settle back onto the sofa. This time our thighs are close, almost touching. He doesn't notice. But I do.

I lift my feet up under me. Half the sofa is completely unoccupied, we're sitting so close. He uses handmade soap that I find for him, free of preservatives, dyes, and anything at all that might be linked to cancer. The science on the whole cause and effect with cancer is sketchy. But I urged him years ago to not take risks. I've helped him pick almost every single item in his home, from cleaning products to shampoo, conditioner, and soap, to the food in his refrigerator. One of the benefits of having such an active role in his product selection is I pick items with scents I like.

The soap he's using right now has rosemary and olive oil in it. The scent is subdued and natural. His V-neck t-shirt reveals his scar. It's a small scar, less than two inches wide, below his collar bone. When he goes to work, he covers it. I suspect I might be the only person he reveals it to. Not that anyone would flinch. He simply doesn't want to answer questions. Most people don't know what that scar means, and they'd ask innocently enough, expecting some story about a skateboarding accident or falling out of a tree as a kid. Or maybe people just don't think when they ask about the origin of scars.

His hand falls to my thigh. It's casual. Friendly. He's watching straight ahead, unaware of what his touch on my thigh does to me. Unaware that I'm not watching the television at all. That I don't care deeply about Noah and Allison. Unaware that the only reason I cry at the end is that deep down I'm seeing the two of us, after decades together, sharing our love story in a notebook.

I lean into him and rest against his chest. He wraps his arm around me, pulling me close. His focus is on the television. He's touching me absentmindedly, while I'm hyper-aware of every breath, the dim beat of his heart, the sprinkling of auburn hair dusting his forearms, the line of his jaw. The light reflects on the stubble scattered across his jaw and the top of his throat, casting a mixture of copper and chestnut hues. I want to lean in and press my lips to his throat, to nuzzle his day-old growth.

Being relegated to best friend status is its own special kind of hell. The friend zone. A bittersweet holding cell with a lifetime penalty.

The television blares louder with a commercial. He squeezes my thigh. "Do you want some more wine?"

"Sure."

I push forward to stand at the same time he does, and we face each other, inches apart. When I tilt my head up, he looks down, and our lips are so close. A few inches is all it would take.

He shakes his head with a low, guttural groan, a sound I'm not sure he knows he made, and pushes me down on the sofa.

"I'll get it. Sit here."

He brings the bottle back and pours more. We are on the brink of finishing off two bottles tonight. Not unheard of by any means, but unusual for us on a Monday.

My phone buzzes, and I lean over for it.

> **Yara**
> David is here. Come out!

"You still seeing David?" Jason's question is quick, and his tone rings with surprise.

I drop the phone and slide back on the seat, deciding I'll respond to Yara later. "No. Not since the night you and Yara joined us."

I set my wine glass down on the coffee table and reach for the throw Jason has crammed on the far end of the sofa. As I'm pulling it over my legs, Jason sets his glass down and pulls me into our favorite sofa position. He lies down flat and aligns my body next to his. There's nothing better than this. Cocooned on the cushions with his warmth surrounding me.

His hand drifts to my stomach, beneath my sweater, on my exposed skin. His fingers trace the curves of my waist, caressing, transmitting flutters of electricity throughout my torso. I shift my hips back against his in reaction, slow, subtle. I need to hide how turned on I am right now. I don't want him to think we can't hang like this, because I love it so much.

He drifts higher, and his fingers touch the wire on my bra. I catch my breath. Does he know? Did he mean to go that high?

I shift my hips again, pressing back on his groin.

He ventures higher, grazing my breast. I freeze. He could be absentmindedly touching me, engrossed in whatever we are watching. He might not even be aware. But it feels so good, so intimate, I don't want him to stop. If he's not aware, I don't want realization to hit.

Then there is the unmistakable warmth of his skin against my bare breast, and his thumb brushes across my nipple. He's shifted the lace cup of my bra down so he can fondle my breast.

I rotate back to give him better access. His lips fall to mine. I roll onto my back, and he moves so he's lying between my legs.

The energy shifts and it's as if someone lit a match and set a timer, telling us we have a limited amount of time before the fire extinguishes.

He unbuttons my jeans as I reach for his. He breaks our kiss long enough to remove my sweater and send it sailing across the room. I reach for his shirt and pull it over his head. Then his mouth is back on mine as we both squirm, pushing our jeans down. When he slides inside and takes me, I gasp. I try to spread wider to wrap my legs around him, but

I can't because my jeans are shoved down, crowded around my ankles, trapping my legs.

And I don't care at all because right now, the man I love is inside me, filling me, and the experience is astounding. We move together, groaning, and I don't want it to ever stop. But then his hand drifts between us, and his mouth falls to my nipple, and the combination of his hand and his mouth and the sensation of him filling me is too much, and my toes curl as my muscles contract, milking him. He stills, and I watch as his face contorts as he loses control, his thrusts becoming erratic as he groans and releases within me.

I kiss down the line of his jaw until his lips return to mine, and our tongues dance, slower now. When he pulls out, he grimaces. Then he collapses beside me, as he once again caresses my belly and my breasts. The moment is intimate and in some ways perfect. He places a soft kiss on each of my nipples then slings his feet, tethered together by his jeans, onto the floor.

He stands and pulls the jeans up before heading in the direction of the bathroom.

I might suspect I dreamed the entire episode, except I'm lying naked with my jeans around my ankles and the blanket is now on the floor. Oh, and his cum is leaking out of me. Lovely. I pull my bra cups back over my breasts and sling my feet onto the floor, much the same way he did, and pull my jeans up.

I'm pulling my sweater over my head when he comes out of the bathroom. We face each other. Inside, I'm quaking. Scared about what he might say. Hopeful this is the turning point for us. That he's going to want more than friendship. That I can have it all with my best friend.

When I study his stance, hunched shoulders, and bowed

head, it's too much. His stoic expression says everything. I step around him. He doesn't say a word. In his small bathroom, I take in my image in the mirror. My hair has the just-fucked look, not matted but frantic disarray. I run my fingers through my hair to calm it down. My cheeks are flushed, and my eyes have a glassy appearance. I will not cry. I grab some pieces of toilet paper to blot them. I don't want the telltale sign that I've been crying, the swollen red skin on my cheeks. I take my time in the bathroom. When I've sufficiently gathered myself, I open the door and head out into the den.

I walk straight to the entry, where my shoes, pocketbook, and coat lie in a heap on the floor. "It's late. I'm going to head on home." I keep my voice casual, upbeat. I can't let him know I'm emotional. If he senses I'm emotional, he won't let this happen. Maybe I don't want it to happen anymore. But leaving the door open feels vital.

He's in the kitchen, rinsing our wine glasses. He glances over his shoulder and calls out, "Be safe. Text me to let me know you got home okay?"

As soon as the door closes behind me, the tears freefall. *What the fuck am I doing?*

When I get home, I text him that I'm back safe. Then I take a long, scalding shower. I'm such a fucking moron. Maybe…maybe this is just the normal transition of awkwardness, from best friends to something more? Maybe if we do this enough, one day it will become our normal, and without any conversation, we'll just be more? Or maybe this confirms he's viewing this as friends with benefits? He definitely didn't seem to want to cuddle afterward. Aside from our friendship, what are we doing?

I'm not on the pill, and I told him I'd start it. I dropped it years ago because my lack of love life made it feel like a waste of money and needlessly dumping chemicals into my body. Crap. I will call the gynecologist tomorrow and make an appointment. While we are in the throes of whatever the hell is going on, I should at least take some responsible steps.

I get into bed and pick up my phone to put it on the charger.

Jason
Hey, I've been reviewing the financials you sent to me. Things aren't adding up. And by the way, do you guys actually give any money to research? Or anything? I don't see it in here. I'll bring lunch to your office tomorrow, and we can go over this. Text me what you're in the mood for in the morning. 12:30? I'll bring your flowers too.

He's so good about that. He noticed that I love fresh flowers in my office years ago. And he brings fresh flowers by pretty much every week, either on Monday or Tuesday. He's bought me several different vases. If a vase at the office gets too dirty because it's hard to clean in the office bathroom sink, he'll switch it out with a fresh vase and bring the dirty vase home with him to clean. Therese calls him my flower guy.

It is incredibly sweet. He's incredibly sweet. And that's why I'm incredibly confused.

twenty-one

Jason

Maggie sits in the back of the cab, scrolling through email. She's wearing a form-fitting brown turtleneck, black slacks, and heeled, pointed black boots. She pulled her long brown hair up into a ponytail within minutes of sliding into the back of the cab. She does that throughout the day. Pulls her hair up, then lets it down, then pulls it up, then lets it down.

Sometimes, for the hell of it, I count how many times she does this. If she's sleeping on the sofa, I count her freckles. Fifty-nine freckles lightly scattered across her cheeks. She currently has thirty-five handbags. That's a weird one to keep track of, I know. But she buys them in thrift stores and random places and tends to use the same one for months on end until she wants to switch it out. She stores them at the top of her closet, and that's where I come in. I'll stand on a step stool and pass her boxes down to rummage through when she's hunting for a particular one or simply in the mood for a change. I'm a numbers guy. So, of course, I count.

Lunch today went well. It wasn't awkward. Until Jane, her boss came in when I was helping her calculate the year to date values she needed for the grant she's working on. Maggie looked like she had been caught doing something illegal. My gut instinct tells me the charity she works for isn't on the up and up. Maggie says I'm only suspicious because the charity was started by Senator McLoughlin, and I disagree with his politics.

I do disagree with his politics. I think he's all about money and not about people, but to be fair, that's my view on most politicians. Still, numbers don't lie. After Jane left her office, Maggie frowned and told me she'd get the numbers she needed from Jane, and I didn't need to do anything else. Fine. I don't know why she didn't go to Jane in the first place.

When I left Maggie's office, she didn't seem pleased with me. So, when Sam's assistant, Janet, called with an invitation for dinner with Sam tonight, I jumped at the chance. It meant more time to smooth over whatever tension is going on between us. I knew she'd agree to go out because she never turns down dinner with Sam. When Sam gets dinner reservations, it's for places with good food, and he always picks up the tab. For years, I tried to pay. But at a certain point, you accept your friend is a billionaire, and you let him cover the tab.

Sam orders phenomenal wines. It's not like I struggle financially. I do well enough as an assistant professor, especially when you consider I have the life insurance from my parents plus their estate. But I don't order the kind of wines Sam does. I'd never, and I mean never, drop the kind of cash Sam drops on a meal out.

Maggie continues scrolling on her phone, acting as if whatever she's reading is fascinating. Maybe it is. Fine by me. It gives me the opportunity to look at her without her realizing it. I love looking at her. Observing her. I notice if she gets a new lipstick shade. Or if she paints her nails a different color. If she buys any new item of clothing, I notice. Because I've memorized her entire wardrobe. She's beautiful. Natural in a small-town girl kind of way, utterly unique in this soot-covered city.

I shouldn't have done anything with her last night. Or that day in her apartment. Or even the night we were both so incredibly drunk I only remember the night in flash frames. But it's as if now that we've opened Pandora's box, I can't close it. Last night, something snapped, and I had to be inside her once again. I love her with every bit of my soul. I love her so much, that no matter how much it hurts, I will not let her fall for me. So, I'll be a jerk. Make her think I'm hooking up with other women. Whatever it takes. She deserves a life I can't give her.

The blasted image of her standing by Adam's graveside comes to mind whenever I contemplate more. It's a photograph in my memory bank, and my mind pushes it forward every time I ponder the life I want for Maggie. It's as if there's a person in charge of the images, and at the first hint of me growing weak, he says, "Oh, no, not now. Don't forget the funeral!" and he propels it forward, center spot, so instead of passing shops or pedestrians or restaurants, I see Maggie's back, alone, standing by Adam's grave. *Yes, brain. That is what I don't want for her. Got it.*

When we arrive at our destination downtown, I swipe Maggie's proffered cash away, pay for the fare, and follow her inside.

Carbone's is one of my favorite Italian restaurants in the city. Sam chooses this place at least once a month. I don't check in with the hostess, because I know Sam's already at our table. It's a small round table in the corner. The brick walls provide the character, as does the artwork on the walls. But it's the food that keeps us coming back.

"How're ya'll?" Sam asks, his southern twang coming out in his words. He works to hide his Texan accent, but at times, when he's trying to welcome someone, or calm a tense situation, he brings out his southern roots. I'm not sure he knows when he does it.

Maggie answers him and glances to me for agreement with her statement. Yes, we're doing fine. She and I are doing fine.

I take her coat and pull out her chair for her to take a seat. I caress her back as she sits. Her startled eyes are the only reason it crosses my mind that the gesture might be too much. In the past, she wouldn't think twice about it. But with the recent slips, maybe that's changing.

When I return from coat check, Sam and Maggie are already deep in conversation. Maggie is like that. She can talk to anyone. I suppose I could too, but I seldom want to. On a night like this, I far prefer to sit back, watch her, and listen. Maggie's from the Midwest, and as such, doesn't have a distinctive accent. Or at least, it's not one that's easy to mimic. She has a sweet-sounding voice that wraps me up like a lullaby. I don't think I'll ever get tired of listening to her talk. Man, can she sing. If she drinks enough on karaoke night, she'll belt her favorite songs, and the whole place pauses to listen. Not to laugh, but to appreciate her.

"So, have you guys decided what you're doing over Christmas? Are you going skiing?" Sam hits my arm when he asks the question after our dinner has been set out before us. I must have been zoning out. I tend to do that.

"We haven't talked about it." I toy with my fork to avoid Maggie's gaze. I was going to talk to her, but then the massage incident happened, and I didn't want wires to get crossed. Given what happened last night, today's probably not a good time to discuss spending Christmas vacation together either.

I stare at Sam in an attempt to silently communicate with my adopted brother. He should change the subject.

Maggie kicks my shoe under the table and asks "What's wrong with you?"

My attempt may have come off as some sort of a scowl. My expressions don't always correctly translate.

"Nothing." I sip my wine. I'm not going to get into this with Sam here with us.

"Maggie, bless your heart for putting up with this guy. I don't know how you do it."

She graciously smiles. If you listened to Sam, you'd assume Maggie and I are together. That's not okay. The next chance I get, I need to make sure Sam knows not to make statements like that. Statements that twist reality into us being a couple. He knows we're just friends, but it's statements like that that could confuse things between Maggie and me. We don't need that right now.

I focus on the meal in front of me. The menu here is fantastic, but tonight, I chose an old favorite, the spicy rigatoni. The pasta here is homemade and always cooked to perfection, and the vodka sauce reminds me of the sauce my mom used to serve. I can remember her twisting the green lid off the jar when she'd make dinner for us. Her sauce wasn't homemade, and so many times I've tried to remember what brand she used. I've bought almost every marinara sauce on the grocery store shelves in my quest. No luck.

Maggie ordered her favorite too, the veal parmigiana. She cuts a small piece and offers me a bite. I accept, and she places her fork in my mouth. I close my eyes to fully appreciate it. It's the flavors that come through that set the food at Carbone's apart from other Italian restaurants, and perhaps what makes this the home of a Michelin chef.

"How's the semester going?" Sam asks.

"Fine," I answer. "How's work going for you these days?"

"It's good. We've got a new batch of interns starting. It's not in the news yet, but I'm going to make that change I told you about. Shift my focus to the VC side. I've put all the wheels in place. I'm ready."

"You know, it's mind-blowing what you've done with the company. And to think I'm your drinking buddy."

"You earned your PhD, Jason. I'd say you've accomplished a lot too," Maggie adds. When she looks at me with those doe eyes, in the way she's looking at me right now, like I hung the moon, it batters home how much of a heel I am, and how much I don't deserve her friendship. She always, no matter what, sees good things in me. It's unfathomable.

"One of these days, I want what you two have," Sam says out of nowhere, wistful.

"What are you talking about?" I ask. Maggie and I aren't together.

"She stood by you through grad school, through chemo, and hospital stays." I push my plate away, full, unable to take anymore, as he continues. "And you are always hanging out waiting for her to finish her volunteer shifts, cheering for her during whatever marathon or century ride she's signed up for. You guys pull for each other, you're each other's cheerleaders. It's got to be nice to have someone like that."

Maggie's cheeks flush, and she reaches for my hand underneath the table to squeeze it. I let her, but the moment lasts too long, and I withdraw my hand and reach for my water glass. None of this is good. I feel it in my chest, a tightness. Sam doesn't know it, but all his talk makes it harder, and it confuses what's already a muddled mess between Maggie and me.

"You used to have lady friends by the dozen." I throw that in not because I believe it's true, but it's how we give Sam shit, and I need to change this conversation.

"You know better."

"Read about it on *Page Six*."

"You know better than that, Jason." Maggie scolds me with a frown. "Sam, if I set you up on a date, would you go?"

"No." His response is so quick I laugh.

Maggie rolls her eyes. Next thing I know, Maggie is getting updates on Sam's family. I find I'm hungry again.

When we've finished dinner, Sam drops a motherload of a bomb when he says, "I have a driver coming by to take y'all back to your place."

"Sam, that's not necessary. You've already paid for our meal like you always do," Maggie tells him, speaking for us.

Once again, he treats us like we're a couple. And Maggie doesn't even correct him. I am screwing this up royally. We're not a couple, and I can't have her thinking that. Acting like we are isn't good for anyone, especially Maggie.

The check arrives, and as Sam pays, I excuse myself and step up to the bar. I need a break from my table and all the hidden innuendos. There are a few stools.

It's not a big bar, but there's a woman sitting at it, eating by herself, so I sit down beside her and order a gin and tonic. I've had too much wine. I need something cleaner and more refreshing.

She looks familiar, and then it hits me. She was in the MFA program when I was getting my doctorate. I don't remember her name, but I remember her face. She fills me in on her life now.

Sam's hand taps my shoulder from behind me. "Hey, we're about to head out. You staying here? You want me to send Maggie home on her own? I can have the driver take her."

Maggie stands several feet back. Sam speaks in a lower tone, so Maggie can't hear. Maybe he's not assuming everything I think he is. Maybe some of it's in my head. But then Maggie looks our way, and I swear, she looks almost angry. As if I shouldn't be talking to a woman. And that's exactly what I can't have. I can't have her thinking she and I are in a relationship. That she has a right to get angry if I'm with another woman. We've got a long history of our friendship withstanding us dating other people. And that's the way it needs to be. For her sake.

"Yeah, that would be great. Thanks."

Sam looks pensive. Judgmental. I brace for him to say something, to tell me I'm an ass, but instead he gives a cursory nod to the woman I'm sitting beside, then he guides Maggie out of the restaurant with his arm on her back.

He'll make sure she gets home safe.

The woman I'm talking to offers to buy me an additional drink, but I decline. I've had far too much tonight.

I keep an eye on my watch. As soon as five minutes have passed, and I know Maggie and Sam will both be in transit home, I tell the woman it was good to see her again. Then I get my coat and step outside to hail a cab.

twenty-two

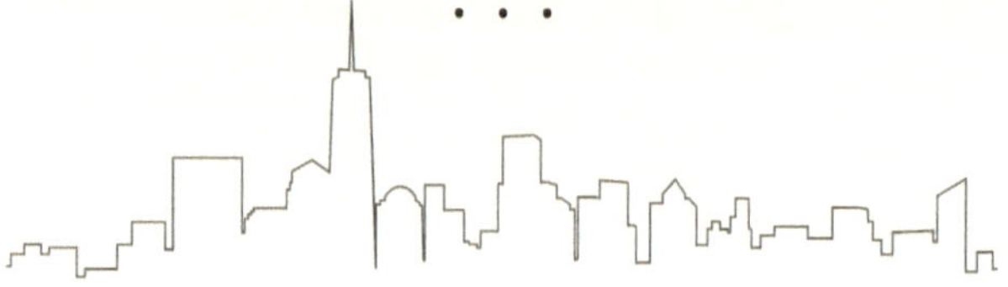

Maggie

"Morning, girl. I made you coffee." Yara greets me in a giant sleep shirt that falls to her knees and super thick socks with a mouse face and yarn balls for ears on each foot. Her hair is a matted mess and leaves little doubt that she, unlike me, got some action last night.

"Thanks."

As she pours a third mug of coffee, I consider telling her what happened last night. That Jason hooked up with a woman at a bar. Not even a bar, really. We were in a restaurant.

She's almost finished doctoring the third cup of coffee when it occurs to me to ask, "So, did someone stay over?"

Yara glows, and the smile that spreads across her face might be the happiest I've seen on her in eons. I raise my eyebrows and mirror her smile to encourage her to say more.

"She's pretty awesome."

I sip my coffee and smile at my friend. She's been through a long string of hook-ups without any great meaning behind them, so I'm genuinely happy for her. "Maybe we can all go to dinner tonight? I'd like to get to know her."

Yara lifts both mugs of coffee. "I'll ask her. I mean, you know, it's still new. But this has potential. It's a good thing. It feels good to have potential."

Her words are still running through my head when I flip the light on in my office. I'm happy for my roommate, but damn, I wish I too had potential. Every time I imagine there might be potential with Jason, he proves there's none. It's like slamming my head up against a wall and hoping each time it won't hurt as much the next time I do it. He's made it abundantly clear he only wants a friendship. If I had any doubt, him picking up girls in front of me sort of proves it. And the thing is, I'm so mortified by the entire situation, I can't bring myself to tell anyone about it.

There's really no point in telling anyone, anyway. I already know what they'd say. My sister would tell me to stop hanging out with him, maybe move back home, and Yara would tell me to stay the hell away from him. Since I can hear them in my head, there's no reason to play the live audio.

I'm in the middle of responding to an email when there's a tap on the doorframe to my office. Jane closes the door, and in two quick strides is at my office chair. I can tell from her imposing height over my desk she's wearing tall heels today or possibly platform heels. There's a scowl on her face that means she's pissed.

I stop typing and rotate my chair to face her. Something is seriously wrong.

"Did you give Jason access to our database?" Her nails flutter against the fabric of the office chair.

"No."

She arches an eyebrow, clearly not believing me.

"I didn't. I printed out some pages. Results from the first half of the year."

"I told you not to share that information with anyone. Those figures are not public. And what you shared with him isn't even accurate. That's why I asked you. No, I told you not to share incomplete information. Private data."

"I only asked him to help me figure out some of the data for the Prospect grant. That's it."

"If you need information, you ask me. Do you understand?"

"Yes."

She glares at me in a way that makes me feel like I've somehow personally attacked her. My boss has never been this angry at me before.

"Send me an email with exactly what you need, and I'll get you the information by the end of this week. This is your warning. If you share private information again…"

She doesn't finish the statement, but from her scowl and overall posture, there is no doubt what will happen. She huffs dramatically, in what seems to be her transition from angry boss to congenial boss, then sits down in the chair.

"Can you give me a quick rundown of what remaining grants must be completed for this year and the first quarter next year?"

We go over my status sheet each week. I hand her a clean copy I had printed for the meeting we're supposed to have on Friday during my one-on-one meeting with her. She asks a few more questions than normal, and it feels like maybe she's trying to make up for jumping down my throat.

Jane has a reputation for being a ball buster. I don't mind. That's how she's so good at her job, and how she got picked by Senator McLoughlin to run his charity. It annoys me to no end that women who are good at their job often get labeled a bitch. Sometimes you just have to cut through the crap to get things done. Men acting the same way are admired. Women are considered menopausal.

By the time she leaves my office, we're back on cordial terms. I'll have the data to get the grant submitted by the end of the week. All is good.

Then the phone rings. I see the digits displayed on my office phone screen and debate answering. After the third ring, I pick up.

"Hey, Zo," I call her Zo, and she calls me Mags. She's my sister, and I suppose she's my real best friend. Or she was my other best friend.

"What's wrong?" That's my sister. I utter two words and she's got a barometer on my mood.

"Nothing."

"Mags." She's using her stern voice, the tone that says *don't bullshit me.*

Tears form, and I stare out my office door at the blank beige wall my office opens onto, considering if I should get up and close the door. "Jason hooked up with someone last night."

"Okay." There's hesitation in her tone. What she's saying in the slow way she utters the word is *And why is this a problem? The two of you are just friends, and he's made this abundantly clear time and time again, you imbecile.*

One tear glides down my cheek, and I swipe it away. That

is all I will allow myself. Zoe's right. I deserve this. I am the imbecile.

"How are you doing?" Her question lacks any accusation at all, just concern. Which I kind of hate, because now I'm really tearing up. I suck air through my nose, determined to keep it under control. I will not cry. Not at work.

"Mags…I know it hurts. But it was bound to happen eventually."

She can't see me, but I still nod, hands balled into fists, as I continue to suck air in through my nostrils and exhale with determination.

"Why don't you come home and visit? I could use your help preparing for Mom and Dad's anniversary. I have this dream of finishing a video montage, and you are way better at that than I am. And Natalie misses her Aunt Mags. She wants to bake a cake with you."

I look up to the ceiling, swiping the soft skin above my cheekbones, swallow, breathe, and say, "I'll look into flights. It would be good to see you guys."

twenty-three

Jason

I need to complete the statistical analysis for a project, grade a stack of projects, and draft an article. The only problem is that I keep staring at my laptop. This is such bullshit.

Maggie isn't responding to my texts. I pushed it too far with her. Had no business blurring our friendship lines. She's better off without me. I know that. It doesn't mean it doesn't absolutely suck.

There's a tap and the door to my office, which had been set ajar, swings wide. Sam enters. "Hey, man!"

He's all bright and cheerful, the way I guess someone who played around with some code and ended up with a billion dollars in his bank account would be. He plops down into one of the ancient wooden chairs across from my desk.

"I thought we were meeting at six-thirty? At the restaurant." Yes, I could have fucked up, but I don't think so. I spoke to Janet a few hours ago.

"Yep, that was the plan. But I wanted to get out of my office. Figured I'd come down and see if I could convince you to swing by Ten Twenty for a drink before dinner."

I haven't finished a damn thing today. I've started on a few things. Can't focus. I want to curl up in a fetal position. I'm checking the time, thinking about all the shit I still have to do, when he continues in his chipper-ass voice. "If you need to stay here and finish grading papers, that's fine. I have my laptop with me. I can work right from here, and we can head over to Pisticci's whenever you're ready."

A bar might work.

"Someone's been messing with your nameplate, man."

What the fuck is he talking about?

He flips my desk nameplate around. Someone has penciled in the indented letters, coloring in the white areas. Whatever. "Probably a student. Probably did it while I was sitting right here talking to them, and I didn't even realize it." Fuck. I know why he's up here earlier than planned. "If you're here to find out if I've gotten the results back, I haven't. I promise I'll tell you when I do. Should be any day."

"Hey, man, I know you'll tell me. You seemed a little down, so I thought my smiling face might cheer you up."

What I'd really like to do is smack his face. Somehow, smacking the smiling pretty boy would make me feel better. But that feeling is wrong. Sam's like family, and I should be grateful someone out there cares. "You don't need to worry about me. There's nothing you can do, anyway, so don't expend the energy." Really. I'm in a no-win situation here.

"Are you out of your goddamn mind? That makes no sense."

I stare at the books stacked along my wall. One day, I'll get a bookcase. Maybe. Piling everything up on the floor works too. Sam's here because he's worried about the results I don't have yet, but if he keeps pushing, we'll end up talking about Maggie. Cancer's a better conversation topic, and everyone knows that topic sucks.

"Enough about me." I tap my desk with my knuckle as this suffocating sensation overwhelms me, the pain in my chest so intense I don't see a way out. It's as if I'm snorkeling, peering up at the light above, but someone's holding on to my fins, preventing me from reaching the air above. Sam sits forward, poised to ask questions.

"Really. Enough. Can we not talk about me tonight? Please?"

"You got it, man." There's a pause, and I stare at my computer screen. Then my to-do list scribbled down on my notebook.

"Did you know one of your students is an intern of mine?"

I didn't know that, no. I don't actually know what my students do outside of class. *Why would I?*

"Olivia Grayson. Do you know her?"

The name does ring a bell. She comes to my office hours each week. She's pretty much completely clueless. I'll be shocked if she gets better than a C in my class. *Fuck.* Sam would not ask me to help her with her grade, would he? Why would he give a shit what grades his intern makes?

"Yeah, I know her."

We sit staring at each other. There's no fucking way I'm changing her grades for him.

"What's she like?" He has this boyish grin on his face like we're sitting here gossiping or some nonsense.

Wait a minute. "Is that why you're asking me about her? I

thought you might be preparing to ask me to do something nefarious."

Sam laughs out loud, and the sound echoes against the empty walls of my office. "Nefarious? What the…? What do you mean by that?"

"She's having trouble with accounting." Holy shit. It's been a while since I've seen Sam in action. "You planning to hit on your intern?"

"That sounds bad, doesn't it?" He's got this cat-ate-the-canary grin. "She's not actually my intern. We hired her, but she quit. Turns out she took a job working for one of the law firms I work with. Small fucking world, huh?"

"Yeah. But you have connections with half the law firms in Manhattan. I guess odds were she'd end up working with one that's associated with you in some capacity."

He points at me as if I've said something inaccurate. I haven't. I don't play with numbers. "That is a huge exaggeration."

"I doubt it. Anyway, you asked about her. She's smart. Good student. Doesn't have an accounting background. I haven't paid much attention to her, but now that I know she's your love interest, I will."

"Well, I've only asked her out on a date. And when I did, she told me she was busy. All fucking weekend. I asked her out on a Monday."

Look at that. I'm not the only one whose love life sucks these days. "You losing your charm?"

"Nah. I've still got game. And you know me. I love a challenge. I'll float some date ideas by you over dinner. I'll get her to give me a chance. Eventually. I'm not one to give up."

I stare at the crap I have to do on my to-do list. Half-cocked draft articles, mid-development projects, and shit I need to grade. But I'm not in the right frame of mind. I pack up for the day so Sam and I can get out of my depressing-as-fuck office. Still no text from Maggie. I'll give her some space and reach out tomorrow. And in the meantime, I'll let Sam entertain me with his plans for his intern. Anything to get my mind off my life.

twenty-four

Maggie

Jason
Mexican or Indian tonight?

The text comes through on my computer screen as I'm preparing to walk out the door. Jane left for Chicago this morning and won't be back in the office until Monday. She travels to Chicago about every other week to meet with Senator McLoughlin or someone on his team. I like my boss, but it's glorious when she's out of the office.

It's not like we all slack off or don't work, but there's a lightness in the air. A willingness to get together with colleagues for lunch or spend a little extra time chatting in each other's offices.

Today, I kept my door mostly closed to maximize productivity. I'm now fully caught up on everything on my to-do list. At this moment, I'm so caught up my inbox is at zero, my desktop clear, and every electronic document is filed away neatly into folders. I normally obtain this level of absolute organization only during the holidays, when everything in the office crawls to a halt.

I pull my phone off the charger and read the text again. Zoe's and Yara's voices merge in my head. *He's never gonna want more than friendship. You're never going to meet someone else if you're always with him.*

The trouble with having good friends who know you well is that they tell you what you need to hear, even if you don't want to hear it.

Here's the thing, though. I haven't told them everything. Yara knows some of it, but she doesn't know how intense the attraction is. I'd convinced myself it was one-sided, but haven't the last couple of weeks shown he's feeling it too?

In my heart of hearts, I don't believe he really cared for the woman at the bar. I've thought about her, and about what he must have been attracted to. She had blonde hair with dark roots. She was eating at the bar by herself. It made me guess maybe she's a business traveler, staying in a nearby hotel. I created an entire backstory for her and decided she must be from Florida, possibly Miami.

If I'm correct, and she's simply in and out of town, and he's drawn to that, then what does that say? Maybe he's finding women he can't possibly build a relationship with in order to block our relationship from going to the next level? But if so, why? He's never been one to date anyone seriously. Even Natalie, a girl I liked who he dated a bit back when I was dating Dan, never reached girlfriend status. Does he just have a thing against serious relationships?

I don't know. It's becoming highly annoying that I obsess over things like this. Our friendship used to be my foundation, my rock that kept me centered no matter what was going on in my life. And now I don't know what to think. About any of it.

Maybe his preference is blonde. Maybe she's into kink. Maybe I'm too vanilla, too plain. Maybe he doesn't know how to tell me all the stuff he's into. Maybe that's why he was so enthralled when I was reading *Fifty Shades of Grey*. He wanted to know how I was reacting to that world, and if it intrigued me. And there I was, blushing and telling him to go away so I could read my book. And then he met the blonde, and she's into what he's into.

I need to forget about the blonde. I need to stop thinking about this. I need to focus on our friendship and finding someone else to help me not think about Jason. But I'm curious. I just need to know about the blonde.

> **Maggie**
> How did things go with the woman from the bar?

I press send, and a cold foreboding shoots through me. Shit! That's out of the blue. What the hell was I thinking? I should have responded about dinner, then segue. He'll read this as anger. Why is there no option to delete a text? Surely, they have the technology.

Three dots float, and I wait. Jason doesn't examine things the way I do. It's possible he won't think twice about it.

> **Jason**
> Good. She went to Columbia. Friends in common.

I chew the corner of my thumbnail. Maybe he wasn't really hitting on her? Maybe she's just a friend. But no, that doesn't make sense. Not the way Sam acted that night. And Jason didn't introduce me to her. It's still possible she's a business traveler.

Maggie
Nice. You going to see her again?

There. I rest my phone on my desk. Good response. It's casual. It's what a friend would ask a friend. I hold my breath, transfixed by the three dots.

Jason
Yes. Definitely.

Salty tears sting my eyes, and I throw my phone into my pocketbook. I'm all caught up, so I have zero work to bring home. I don't want to go home to an empty apartment, or worse, to an apartment filled with the giggles and flirty glances of new budding love. I am happy for Yara, but I'm not in the state of mind to participate in her happiness.

So, I head to Bellevue. It's not my evening to volunteer, but there will probably be something I can do. Even if it's simply to play a game of RubiCube or spades or Mancala In the evening hours, there's always someone who doesn't have a visitor and needs something other than the mind-numbing blue tube.

My ring tone sounds as I'm entering the hospital's sliding glass doors. The bright modern interior with graphic city illustrations on the back wall convey a joy I don't feel. My ringtone is loud. I have to answer.

"So, you never answered me. What kind of food do you want me to order?"

I chew on the corner of my lip, annoyed he called. My lack of response should have counted as a response. He can be infuriatingly dense and slow to pick up on the nuances of communication. "I'm sorry. I forgot to respond. I'm volunteering tonight."

"Tonight's not your night."

"I got called in. About to get on an elevator. Talk to you tomorrow?" Then I hang up. I never do that. But there's a first for everything.

twenty-five

Jason

Thick wall-to-wall carpet lines the hall. A slim plate hangs beside each of the four doors down the corridor, identifying the business name and the unit number. There's a dingy smell, the kind of odor that permeates basements in older homes.

Shannon, my therapist, rents this space. It's a creative way to run her own business. Her office is tiny. The bathroom down the hall is shared by all the occupants renting on this floor. It's on Park Avenue, so it has a quality address, but there's nothing particularly upscale about this floor.

The asphyxiating sensation hits full force, to the point I angle my head upward as if I'm literally underwater. I consider twisting the knob on the door. Chest pain radiates. Pressure on my lungs intensifies as if someone is attempting to compress them.

I can't do it. Not today. I called for the appointment. An

emergency after-hours therapist appointment. I'll pay the cancellation fee, but I'm not going in.

Within seconds, the smell of car exhaust greets me as I return to the street. A large city bus rolls along with the tell-tale black smoke from the back of the vehicle coating the street in grime. Somehow, I prefer the polluted air out here to the stifling intensity of the bottom floor of those offices.

This whole night blows. I should be sitting in a restaurant with Maggie. Or on my sofa, curled around her. But she's mad at me. Can't say I blame her. I'm fucking everything up. Sending out mixed signals. I know I can't have her. So why the fuck did I open that door? And keep opening it?

If I don't get my shit together, I'm going to lose her.

It's not until I'm pushing the door to my apartment open and catch the time on my watch that it hits me. It took me over an hour to trek back to my place. I circled the hospital. More than once. Debating surprising her. Offering to play a game with her and the patient. But I figured that would violate volunteer policy. I considered dropping off a hot tea. It can be cold in the hospital, and Maggie often doesn't dress warmly enough when she volunteers. I thought about stopping by to ask when she finishes, so I could walk her home. Or offer to buy her a glass of wine to unwind.

My life sucks. I throw the keys down on my kitchen counter, and they clatter across the tile countertop. The sharp noise ricochets through the empty space.

I haven't had dinner. I should eat. But I'm not hungry. If anything, mild nausea accompanies this suffocating sensation, this tightness and pressure. I'm tired. I am tired of all of this. Feeling like this. Wanting something so badly but knowing doing so would be selfish. Falling in love with one cancer patient and letting them go is more than anyone should have to go through. I can't let Maggie go through that twice. No way, no how.

The apartment is cold. I reach for the neatly folded blanket Maggie set on the sofa and pull it over me. Stare at the ceiling. Avoid the stack of work I brought home. Light filters from outside, along with the low hum of city noise. The sound of an ambulance, a car alarm.

I close my eyes. Breathe.

I find myself in a familiar place, surrounded by snow. A man trudges by in snow boots, carrying a snowboard. Two young girls carrying skis over their shoulder head toward the lift. Sam and Ollie are off in the distance, waving to me to come on.

My mom and dad call me over. They're standing close to me. "Honey, you've been skiing with your friends all week. Are you sure we can't convince you to spend one day with us?"

"Leave him alone. Let them be boys. We'll meet you at The Little Nell. Do you have a credit card?"

Behind me, Sam and Ollie shout, "Come on, man. We've got to meet Paul."

I whip back around, searching for my folks. Mom. No. Please don't. Give me a hug. At least. This time. Stay. Don't go.

I scan the crowd, frantic. I can't find them. I've already lost them.

Then I find them. Both have skis over their shoulders. Walking toward a different lift. They didn't tell me where they were skiing. They always forget to tell me where they're going.

I push off on my right foot, to catch up with them. My foot sinks into the snow. I push down on my left, and it sinks farther down. The snow opens into a hole. The harder I push, the deeper down I sink. No one notices me. No one helps. Conversations buzz around me as everyone heads to their lift.

I need to stop them. This time. I have to stop them.

Snow spills into the hole. All around me. I struggle. It's a sinkhole. "Mom! Dad! I'll go! I'll go! I'll go!" I scream, as loud as I can.

Everything goes dark. The only sound is my rapid breaths. I pat my face. I'm drenched. I swallow. Fuck. I hate my life.

twenty-six

Maggie

"Good morning. Happy Friday!" I singsong to Stephanie with a joy I lack.

This morning, I woke up expecting texts from Jason. Nothing. If I'm honest, I halfway expected him to come over last night. If things are tense with us, he usually shows up. He doesn't like the phone if things are tense. He needs to see me.

Last night, I worked on a puzzle with Shonia. She's a twelve-year-old girl with a ton of spirit, admitted a week ago due to a neutropenic fever. Her mom had been there during the day, but had to head home to get her siblings squared away for the night. Most of the night, she and I talked. Jay-Z. Beyoncé. Ariana Grande. Nail designs and trends. Billie Eilish.

She bounced around topics like a *Teen Vogue* magazine. Or, more accurately, a teen blogger covering all the hot topics of the hour. Without a doubt, we helped each other.

She helped to take my mind off whatever the hell happened between Jason and me, and I kept her from feeling lonely and thinking too much about the unfairness of being sick in a hospital bed at her age.

Hassenfeld Children's Hospital paints the walls bright and cheery. They do what they can. But, no matter how happy they paint it, they can't cover up the unfairness of it all. Seeing what these kids go through always helps me with my perspective. Reminds me of what I have to be grateful for.

I entered that hospital all twisted over a text exchange with Jason. Meanwhile, some of the kids in these walls have terminal illnesses and won't live to drink a cocktail legally. To go to college. To live on their own. Perspective. It does a body good.

I'm cranking up my computer, absorbing my coffee, and reading my to-do list when an unknown number rings.

"Good morning. This is Maggie Thompson."

"Hi. Ms. Thompson, this is Rachel Lee with Chi-Town Recruiters."

"Hello." She's got my attention. She's the first recruiter to ever call me.

"I'm searching to fill a director position at The Health Foundation, and your name was recommended to me. Do you have a moment now to talk?"

"Sure." It never hurts to hear about an opportunity. Although her information must not be too accurate, given I'm not at the director level.

"Great. Are you familiar with The Health Foundation?"

"I am." It's my job to be familiar with most of the top-performing cancer research charity groups.

"Well, your name comes highly recommended for the

director position based on the grants you've submitted on behalf of The McLoughlin Charity. The open director position would be a step up from your current role as an associate. You would manage five employees, and in addition to grant writing, your responsibilities would include managing charity fundraising events. The salary is $115,000."

Holy shit. I currently make $60,000. "The position sounds interesting."

"They'd like to fly you out for interviews as soon as possible. Interviews with other candidates are occurring next week."

And there's the issue. "Where are they based?"

"Chicago."

Somehow, before the end of the phone call, I've agreed to fly out for a Monday interview. She asks if I'd like to fly out this evening or tomorrow morning, to spend time with my family. The family comment throws me, then I remember it's on my bio on our company website. I can hear her fingers tapping away on a keyboard. She says there are still flights available on both the 7:00 p.m. flight this evening and the 9:00 a.m. flight tomorrow.

I text my sister while I'm on the phone with the recruiter.

Zoe
Yes! Come on! I'll pick you up from the airport.

As if. Chicago is a two-hour drive from her house. I'll rent a car. I've been wanting to see her.

I text my boss. Her response is almost instantaneous.

> **Jane**
> No problem. I won't be back in the office
> until Wednesday.

Within a mere ten minutes on the phone, I'm confirmed for weekend plans, and Rachel, the recruiter extraordinaire, promises to email me my interview schedule before the end of the day. Crazy. It's more of a free weekend trip home. There's no way I'll move away from New York. My life is here.

Within minutes of saying goodbye to Rachel, my phone rings, displaying Zoe's number on the screen.

"Hey, lady." I knew she'd call.

"I'm so excited! I texted Will and told him he's on kid duty this weekend."

"Hey, now! I want some Natalie time." My niece is the absolute cutest. Zoe and Will are discussing a sibling for her, and I can't wait. There is absolutely nothing in the world like the smell of baby. Second best is toddler, and that's what my little Natalie is now. She's two and still has plenty of baby fat to squeeze.

"There will be plenty of Nat time. Trust me. Will being on duty hardly means I'm off duty." There's a touch of annoyance in her tone. He's a good guy, but they're among the first of their friends to have kids, and I sense at times they miss their freedom.

"I have an idea. Why don't I babysit Saturday night and let you and Will go out?"

There's a pause. "You'd do that?"

"Of course! I'd love to."

"Maybe we will do that. So, tell me, what's this interview?"

I tell her all about it. "And the salary is one-fifteen."

"What? You mean $115,000? At a non-profit?"

"Yep. I mean, I'm not gonna get it. But, crazy, right? It's not like I'd leave New York, anyway."

"Wait. Stop right there. Why wouldn't you leave New York? The job is doing what you love, making twice as much as you make now, in a city with a fraction of the cost of living. Why, exactly, would you not move?"

"I love New York."

"Uh-huh."

"What does that mean?" I know that tone. She's mastered the art of speaking volumes with her varying versions of 'uh-huh.' Sometimes I feel for Will because he doesn't always register when he needs to be backtracking.

"It has nothing to do with that city. You've told me before you think Chicago's better. You prefer the lake to the brown rivers over there."

I rest my forehead on my hand. She's not wrong. On a different day, I'd change the subject or fight her, but today, I'm beat. There's no fight in me.

"It's Jason." She practically spits out his name. I don't understand the venom. He's a nice guy.

"He's important to me," I say with a defensive tone that I absolutely mean.

"Well, I don't need to remind you that you're thirty-two years old. And you want more than friendship with him, and he doesn't. It's not a healthy place to be in."

"What does my age have to do with it?"

"The clock is ticking!"

"Fuck you."

"I'm serious."

"So am I," I huff. And I'm not thirty-two yet. I have over a month to go. Just because she went and got pregnant on her honeymoon, now she's like this have-a-baby advocate. "Besides, the clock doesn't really start to tick these days until thirty-seven or thirty-eight."

"Who told you that?"

"Just a gazillion bloggers."

"Yeah, a gazillion bloggers who are going to end up adopting. Look, kids or no kids, getting away from him will be good for both of you. You guys are, like, addicted to each other. You can't go out without the other, and all you really want to do is stay in. And news flash. You aren't going to meet another guy sitting on antisocial Jason's sofa."

"He's not antisocial."

"Yes, he is. At the very least, let's agree he's seriously on the far end of the introverted spectrum. Possibly depressed."

"Leave Jason alone."

"Seriously, Jason is fine. He's been your best friend forever, like since I was in junior high. I just want you to have an open mind about moving. I think it would be good for you. You deserve everything you want in life, and I know that includes a husband and kids, and you're not gonna get that with Jason."

I want to argue, but I don't. She's right. She can't resist driving it home when she adds, "He's just not into you that way."

She's wrong, of course. He's proven he's attracted to me. But something's not right. Maybe he doesn't see me as wife material. Maybe he doesn't know how to leave the friend zone.

Maybe, maybe, maybe. I might drive myself crazy with *maybe.*

I leave the office with the intention of heading home,

doing a load of laundry, and packing. Instead, here I am, knocking on Jason's half-cracked open office door. I know his schedule. I have a printout of it on the small corkboard in my office. Each semester, he emails me the schedule, and I switch it out.

He lifts his head and instantly smiles. His reddish hair falls somewhat in place, but toward the back a few strands stick up where he has his cowlick. There's something about that cowlick, the way he can't keep everything buttoned up, that draws me in. Always brings out my smiles.

"Hey. Do you have a few minutes?"

"Yeah. Of course." He pauses, and his brow wrinkles, his concern evident. "Is everything okay?"

I laugh, a mix of awkward and amused. Yeah, he'd be concerned because I rarely, if ever, stop by his office in the middle of the day. He's the one who stops by mine.

"Jane's out of the office."

"Ah. Did she ever get you those numbers you need?"

"She's going to have them to me by the end of the day."

"Well, I'll be glad to look it over."

"Oh, no." I wave my hand in the air as I slump down into his uncomfortable visitor chair. "She made it clear I am not to share anything else with you."

"Don't you find that to be odd?"

I lean forward, considering. "No. Charities come under scrutiny all the time. Especially those run by politicians. As Jane said, our numbers right now are incomplete. If any rumors got started, it could not only hurt our fundraising goals for next year, but it could hurt Senator McLoughlin. And it's normal business practice. No business should be sharing private data." I made a mistake, one I think Jane has forgiven me for. But that's not why I'm here.

"A headhunter called me today." I bounce a bit as I say it. This is my first headhunter call, and it's kind of freaking exciting. "I'm flying out tomorrow morning."

"What? Where's the job?" Jason's pale skin flushes with color and his seat rolls backward from his quick thrust forward.

"Don't worry. I'm not gonna move. But it's a free trip to see Zoe. I've been wanting to spend time with her. The head-hunter offered to fly me out so I could spend the weekend with family and interview on Monday. I'll be back Monday evening."

"What's the job?"

"It's a director level. The Health Foundation. It's all that I'm doing now, plus more. I mean, it's crazy they called me. It's basically Jane's level." A buzz rises as the reality of being considered for a job that's the equivalent of my boss's job surfaces.

"That sounds great, Maggie. Why wouldn't you take it if you got it?"

His question punches me as if he physically reached out and shoved me. I cross my legs and scan the stacks and stacks of books and papers that line his back wall. He needs to spend time filing.

"Maggie." His tone pulls me back to the here and now. "When they meet you, they're going to love you. You've dedi-cated your career to raising money for cancer research. You know the industry inside and out. You've got a Rolodex of contacts that has to be exceptional. You interview well."

"How do you know that?" He's my biggest cheerleader. You'd think he was my parent and not my best friend.

"Because I've prepped you for interviews before. I've watched you when you've done podcasts and newspaper interviews." He makes it sound like I'm a celebrity. I'm not. At all. But we do focus on PR, and every now and then, especially before bigger charity events, I get pulled in to talk about the work our non-profit does.

"Well, they've been interviewing candidates. I have to believe some of those candidates are already at the director level and have management experience."

He pulls on his chin, slipping into thoughtful professor mode. "Maybe. But they're flying you out. They wouldn't do that if they already had the perfect candidate. And it's in Chicago? How did they get your name?"

"I'm not sure. A recruiter called me. She said someone recommended me, but she clearly did some research about me on our website." I have a hefty paragraph on the site, with contact information, in case someone reviewing grant applications wants to learn more about the staff.

He exhales loudly and walks around his desk to sit in his other empty guest chair. "You shouldn't be dismissive of this. It could be a great opportunity. And I don't have a great feeling about where you are now."

"Oh, my god, Jason. You're just saying that because you don't like Senator McLoughlin."

"It's true. He's a schmuck. Lying sack of shit. I'll never vote for the man."

"Well, you can't. He's in Illinois."

"Exactly."

I shake my head at him, grinning. It's been a long time since he poked jabs at McLoughlin. I tend to agree with Jason and probably wouldn't vote for him either, but the man's still kind of an indirect boss. "Anyway, how would I ever leave New York? I can't imagine leaving you." There. It's out there. My truth.

twenty-seven

Jason

"If you moved, I'd move too." Obviously. She needs to pursue this job. Something is off with that charity she's with, and she needs to get the hell out of Dodge. My guess is Senator McLoughlin is using that charity to funnel campaign donations, and that's why Jane reacted the way she did when I looked at their books. Maggie might not be suspicious, but I am.

Anger mounts as I think everything through, growing more certain Maggie isn't working at a legit nonprofit. I pace the room and accidentally kick a pile of papers, scattering them several feet. I really need to throw this shit out, but the blue recycling bins are at the end of the hall, so I keep putting it off.

Maggie stoops to help me reform my piles of papers into a semblance of organization. We're both in a squatting position, our knees almost touching, when she asks, "You'd move if I moved?"

"Of course." There's no question.

"But…"

"But nothing."

"Your job, though?"

I reach out and lift her hair, placing it behind her ear so I can get a better look at her. All her freckles are visible, which means she didn't put much makeup on today. Maybe some blush. I've watched her do her makeup a thousand times. She has different levels of makeup. Today's look takes less than ninety seconds, and it's one of my favorites.

"I'd get another job."

"You're teaching at an Ivy League school!" Her eyebrows shoot up with her exclamation.

I stand and extend a hand to help her up. "So? I don't know if I really like it, anyway. I'd find something else to do. You're passionate about your work. It's more important that you find a place worthy of you and that's going to bring out all your potential."

"And you'd move with me?"

What the hell does she find so difficult to understand about this? Of course I'd move with her. We moved from New Hampshire to New York together.

She reaches up and cups my jaw. Her fingers on my skin feel good. I must lean forward, and I'm not quite sure how it happens, but we're kissing. Her lips are soft. Our kiss is slow, almost dream-like.

She pulls away, and I'm buzzed, off-balance as if I've had a few beers. She pushes my office door closed and flips the lock. The sound of that lock clicking knocks any remaining air right out of my lungs. *Holy shit.*

In a step and a half, she's back in front of me, and I pin her against the wall. In my peripheral vision, I notice another pile of papers cascading across the floor, but she pulls my shirt out of my slacks, and it's as if I've fallen under her spell. There are a hundred reasons, some solid, good reasons we shouldn't be doing this, but right now, I don't care about any of them.

She unbuckles my belt and drops to her knees, and I swear it's as if a fantasy I've had for millennia plays out. My knees go weak when she pulls my cock out, lightly gripping it and stroking. When her warm, wet tongue swipes across me, I plant my palm along the wall to remain standing.

Mind blown. I have no idea how this came to be, but there is no way in hell I'm stopping it. She goes down my shaft, and holy shit, what she does with her tongue. I watch, completely transfixed. The warmth of her mouth feels so much better than in any fantasy I've had of her lips wrapped around me.

My desk has a bunch of crap on it. Nothing that can't be placed in piles again. I can push all that off and clear off a place for her in, I'm estimating, ten seconds. If I pull her off me, but I don't want to stop this. Incredible. She's working me, her head bobbing up and down, and holy fuck, I do not want this to stop. She massages my balls then licks them, almost sending me over the edge, then she resumes working up and down my cock. That familiar tightening at the base of my spine hits, and I barely get the warning out before I'm coming down her throat.

"Fuuuck." So much for sex on the desk. Holy shit, that was fantastic. Over way too quickly. I watch her, mesmerized, as she licks up some of my cum she couldn't swallow, cleaning me up with her tongue as if I'm a lollipop. I'll gladly be her candy any day of the week.

Holy shit. My breathing evens out as she places me back in my boxers and zips up my pants. I stop her hands as she sets about buckling my belt and kiss her, forcing myself upon her, overwhelmed by love for her, amazement and gratitude. Never in my life has anything like this happened to me.

She asks if I can take off this afternoon and hang out while she does laundry. I say yes because right now, I'll do anything she asks. Anything at all.

She reorganizes my paper stacks while I unplug my laptop and throw it into my backpack, along with some blue books I need to go through. It'd be so much easier to grade if I didn't give partial credit and have to figure out exactly how my students screwed up.

We're turning right, headed for the stairs, when a voice calls out my name. I'd normally ignore it and continue down the hall, but I'm with the world's most kind-hearted person.

"Hi, there. How are you?"

Maggie and I are holding hands, something I become aware of when I catch my colleague staring at our intertwined fingers. I let her hand go and re-shift my backpack.

"Good." Now he's focused on Maggie, and I wish I hadn't let her hand go.

"Are you going tonight?" He asks the question while blatantly perusing Maggie.

"To what?" I have no idea what the hell he's talking about. This guy, Thomas, is Mr. Social Coordinator.

"Dean Schlosberger's house? Potluck dinner?" His tone rises at the end of each question, and his expression is one of surprise, as if this is somehow a historic event I should be excited about attending. I'm not. I have a long history of feigning sickness or claiming a packed calendar to avoid faculty events just like this one. Not to mention, the man lives in New Jersey.

"No, I can't make it tonight."

He smiles his annoying smile that he always has splashed on. "You're always busy."

Not really. But for a faculty gathering in New Jersey, I am. But his attention isn't on me. It's on Maggie.

He points an index finger. "I know you. You were in my team-in-training group two years ago. The marathon."

Maggie, of course, smiles from ear to ear. "Yes! I remember you. Thomas, right?"

Of course she knows his name.

They drone on. He hasn't done an event since that one. He's impressed she's doing Ireland.

He hits my arm as if we're pals. "Why haven't you brought Maggie around? I always assumed you were ducking out to avoid all the couples."

I stare off at the ceiling. I wish everyone would drop the couple bullshit. It's annoying, and it makes it harder to keep things on the friend's plane. Not that I'm doing a stellar job of that, given what just happened in my office. My collar tightens around my throat, which is odd because it's not buttoned, but I grab at it anyway and rub my throat.

"Mags and I are just friends. She's prepping for an interview in Chicago." Nausea rises, and I feel like I might vomit. I don't remember eating anything that could have been bad. Maybe I'm coming down with something, like the stomach flu.

"You're moving to Chicago?"

Maggie straightens. She shifts her body so she's practically talking solely to Thomas, as if they're the close friends.

"Well, it's doubtful."

She explains more. My heartrate picks up, and out of habit, I place two fingers on my wrist. I haven't been sleeping well. I never sleep well. It wouldn't be surprising if I'm coming down with something. Flu is also on the rise. The university is like a sewage spill of germs. A ton of college students don't even wash their clothes.

"Maybe next week we can get together?" Thomas's hopeful question catches my attention. What the hell did I miss?

"I'd like that." *She's going on a date?*

They exchange numbers as I go through my backpack, searching for my thermometer. I used to keep one in here, but I haven't been as cautious recently. I haven't been using hand sanitizer either.

Thomas heads down the hall, saying I should come tonight if my plans change. As if I'm going to journey all the way to New Jersey.

"Hey, you know what, I remembered I need to do some shopping. Why don't you stay here? You don't like shopping, and I'd rather not deal with you grumbling as I try on outfits."

"I'm coming." I call after her, but she must not hear me because she doesn't even turn around, just throws her hand up in the air and waves as she hurries away.

I don't grumble when she tries on outfits. But she's gone. Bolted down the stairs. No goodbye. I didn't even get to tell her I'm not feeling well. The nausea diminishes, but I'm still not feeling great.

I follow at a normal pace down the stairs. I'll stop by the pharmacy and pick up some good immune boosters. Give Maggie enough time to do her shopping and get whatever was so important done. Later, I'll stop by to help her pack and prep for her interviews. It's a good plan.

twenty-eight

Maggie

The bright cherry-red painted door swings open as I pull alongside the white picket fence. Several inches of snow blanket the lawn and bushes, giving the entire home a Norman Rockwell worthy backdrop. It's the first snow of the season. It still feels like fall in New York, but Wisconsin is slipping into winter.

My sister stands waving from behind the glass storm door, my niece on her hip She's been tracking my drive from the airport. Of course she has. I want to sit in my rental and absorb the Norman Rockwell curb appeal, but that's not an option today, thanks to my eager hosts. Will, my sister's husband, stands outside near the garage, waving me forward.

My tires crunch over the bump where Will created a small snow hill at the end of his drive. The snow shovel rests propped against the side of the garage, so perhaps he hasn't finished his snow clearing task.

The curb appeal was essentially absent when they purchased this place around four years ago, but they've become home improvement extraordinaires. They added black shutters, the cherry red door, painted the house white, re-landscaped, and added the white painted picket fence, which I contend they will regret when they have to paint it each spring. But now, in the snow, the two-story colonial is Hallmark picture perfect.

"Hey there, big sis." Will gives me a warm hug before popping my trunk open to lift my carry-on out. "Zoe is so excited you're here. You have no idea."

The moment I step in the side door, sweet vanilla cookie aroma mixed with a garlic scent surrounds me. "Aunt Maggie!" my sister belts out with my cuddly niece clapping her hands together and squealing by her side. I hug them both and kick off my boots.

"Are you cooking?"

Natalie answers with a happy "cookeees," and Zoe offers an explanation for the garlic. "I have a pot of grandma's chicken and rice soup on the stove, in case you didn't stop for lunch."

I follow Zoe into the kitchen and spin around, taking in the most recent renovation. "Zoe, this is gorgeous." She's sent photos, but seeing it in person really makes me appreciate the work they've done. They hired someone to replace the cabinet doors, but then they did all the painting, and tile work on the backsplash. They stripped the wood floors and let the white pine shine through. Will built the center island out in the garage, and Zoe stained it. Natalie's toddler art with squiggly lines and handprints covers the top half of the stainless-steel refrigerator, creating a sense of love in the bright white kitchen.

Compared to my cramped New York City apartment kitchen, this room is dream worthy. Each year prior to this one, they've redone one of the bathrooms. Zoe swears that one day they are going to move to a home on the lake, but when I look around, I see so much love, sweat, and tears, plus so many memories, I doubt they'll ever move out of this home. This is where they brought Natalie home from the hospital. I mean, as long as they stay in Madison, I don't see them leaving it.

Mom and Dad would, of course, love for them to return to Cedar Falls. Zoe had planned to do just that, but like many who attend the University of Wisconsin, she decided she didn't want to leave. It's not that Cedar Falls is a bad place. But Madison offers a vibrant college scene and quaint shops and restaurants. Lots of Chicagoans come out for a day trip or as a weekend escape. And, at only two hours away, she can daytrip into Chicago, something that cannot be done from our home in Iowa.

After downing two bowls of my grandmother's coveted garlic-laden chicken and rice soup, I curl up with a blanket in the den, while Zoe and Will carry Natalie up for a nap. Zoe explained to me that on weekends, when Will's home, they like to do nap time together, just like they do bedtime together.

None of the furniture in here really matches. It's a collection of pieces she's found in Goodwill over the years, although most of it is mid-century modern, so there's a sense of cohesion. The walls are painted a stark white, and they seem to blend with the pale gray sky and snow backdrop of the front yard.

The sound of my ringtone for Jason drifts through the house. It's the *House MD* theme song. Back in our later college days and for many years after college, it was one of our favorite shows.

My phone is in my pocketbook, sitting by the side door with my snow boots. I don't have any desire to talk to him, so I pull the blanket up to my chin and close my eyes. He stopped by in the evening to help me pack. As if I needed help.

He didn't do anything wrong, but when he told his colleague he and I were just friends, and he didn't bat an eye when the guy asked me out on a date right in front of him, it felt like he lifted his arm and punched me. I know he'd never intentionally hurt me. And he'd definitely never raise his hand and hit me. But that's how it felt.

In all fairness, he's always been upfront with me. He wants me to find someone who will be good to me. And he doesn't want to be that guy.

I don't know what overcame me in his office. Maybe it was when he said that of course he'd move wherever I did, a depraved sense of hope rose. More and more often, I'm seeing that he's attracted to me. In his office, there was no doubt there was attraction. And he enjoyed what I did. I didn't screw it up. He came, for crying out loud. And I swallowed.

My feet are lifted off the sofa, and Zoe slides beneath them.

"She asleep?"

"Tuckered out. We should have a solid ninety minutes. Would you like an Irish coffee? Or a rosé?"

"I'll have whatever you want."

"Let's do Irish coffee. With the snow outside, that'll be good."

She's halfway across the room when Will's voice echoes

down the hall. "Sit, babe. I'll get it for you guys. Do you want me to get a fire going?"

Zoe singsongs a "yes." He bends down and kisses her, and I swear he moans, just from the soft kiss that grew a bit deeper. They've been married for five years. Sometimes it can be a little tough to be around the two of them, as they are so sweet together. She deserves the happy life she always dreamed of. She's a good soul, my little sis.

"So, tell me about this job," she asks as soon as Will heads off to the kitchen to play bartender.

I've filled her in on what little I know by the time Will returns with our spiked coffees loaded with whipped cream. He leans in front of the fireplace, taking care to place wood in a particular pattern before lighting the kindling.

"Will, you are a dream."

He smiles as he responds, "If I wanna keep her, I've gotta try."

As if my sister is going anywhere. She looks at him as if he's her own special ice cream sundae covered in hot fudge.

"I'm gonna head upstairs to get some work done while you ladies catch up. Text me if you need anything, okay?"

Zoe and Will look into each other's eyes, silently communicating the way couples do.

He's a few steps out in the hall when he calls back, "Don't worry about Natalie. I've got her if she wakes up."

I sigh. "Maybe I should have gone to Wisconsin too. I think I missed the boat."

She sips her coffee with a dreamy expression on her face. It's sweet. Then something changes, because she shifts and goes from dreamy to concerned mama bear in five seconds flat.

"What did Jason do?"

I half laugh. "What do you mean?"

"Something's wrong. I can tell. He didn't come with you. And the only thing that ever gets you down is that jackass. So, spill."

"He didn't do anything."

She kicks her foot right into my thigh, and in response, I launch my heel against whatever body part of hers I can slam into. We glare at each other.

"Don't make me spill my drink," she scolds with an index finger aimed my way.

Tears blur my vision. It's my sister, and I need to get it off my chest. It's time.

"I'm not proud of how I've been acting."

Zoe softens as she waits for more.

"I kicked him out last night." The Irish coffee bears a strong bourbon flavor, and I close my eyes to appreciate it and to avoid my sister's gaze.

"What happened?" She's quiet, a hint of caution in her tone.

"We've been sleeping together." The silence that follows forces me to lift my eyelids and check on Zoe.

"Not surprised." She pushes the blanket off her hip and shifts to cross her legs and face me. "But maybe I am a little. Why did he wait so long to make a move?"

"How do you know he made the move?"

"Because I know you, Mags. You aren't the type of girl who would make the first move. Ever."

Hearing the truth out loud smarts a little and swirls a few other emotions around too. Then I remember yesterday.

"Yesterday, I came on to him." My cheeks warm as the embarrassment of that aftermath hits.

"Wait. Start from the beginning."

So, I tell her. I tell her about the tequila night. About the sofa. The massage at my house. I don't get around to telling her about his office. It's too fresh and too embarrassing.

"Okay. He's clearly attracted to you. Has he given you a reason for not wanting to be more than friends?"

"No. I mean, just that we can't lose our friendship. It means too much." A loud truck rumbles by on the road in front of the house, drawing my attention outside. "I think it all comes down to Adam. I think on some level he still sees me as Adam's girlfriend. And after we fool around, he feels guilty, so then he acts weird."

Zoe halfway closes her eyelids and cocks her head. "Wait. You said you threw him out. Why?"

I bury my face in my hands. "Zoe…it was awful. I kind of got it in my head that if he and I kept hooking up, he'd eventually warm to the idea of us being more, or we'd slip into more, ya' know?"

She nods her understanding.

"Well, yesterday, when I told him about this job opportunity, he told me he'd move for me. He said it as if there was no question. He'd move anywhere I needed to move. Would leave his prestigious job behind in the blink of an eye. And, well, I thought that must mean he sees me as more. But I was so wrong."

"I'm not following. What happened?"

"Well, we fooled around."

"Office sex. Nice."

"Not sex. But…we fooled around."

"Okay. Not comfortable sharing. We'll work on that. And then?"

I roll my eyes, indignant at being poked and prodded for more information.

"When we left, we ran into one of his colleagues. Turns out, I know the guy. He was in one of my training groups a couple of years ago."

"And?"

"And nothing. He asked if we were dating, and Jason answered truthfully. He said we were just friends. Then he stood there emotionless as the guy asked me out on a date. Seriously, no emotion whatsoever. If a girl comes on to Jason in front of me, it slices me. I'm sure I'm like an open book too. Like everyone knows. And Jason…he's got red hair! When he's upset, it shows. You can see it. Nothing. Nada. Couldn't have cared less. Pale skin, no color. Moments before, he and I were together. I thought we were progressing, but no. I mean, I could tell him I want a friend with benefits arrangement, and he'd probably agree, but it would never, ever go anywhere."

A lone tear escapes down my cheek as Zoe wraps her hand around mine.

"You haven't finished your story. What happened that made you kick him out?"

"He came over later, uninvited, and acted like everything was normal. I almost ran away from him after we bumped into that guy, and Jason didn't even notice. He let himself into my apartment, announced he'd ordered pizza, and asked if I minded if he turned on the TV while I finished packing. Like nothing at all happened. But here's the thing, Zoe, nothing happened. It's all in my head. He hasn't done anything wrong. I'm the one who's emotional. And it's making me treat him horribly. But, I can't—"

"What did he say when you kicked him out?"

I think back. Shameful. Because I didn't kick him out. Not really. I should have. And, in my way, I did. I told him it was time for me to go to bed. He responded that he wasn't feeling great and said goodnight. I should've kicked him out. I should've stood up for myself. But…

Zoe taps my leg. "Huh?"

"He didn't really say anything."

"He may not have said anything, but he's done plenty. If he wants only a friendship with you, he shouldn't be taking advantage of you sexually. He clearly knows you want more, and he's not being mindful of your feelings. He's not treating you like a friend. That guy is an ass. And I don't know why you've put up with him for so long. But it's like you can't say no to him. Honey, it is time to move on. Move to Chicago and tell him hell no, he can't follow you. You need space away from him."

"This is why I didn't tell you. I knew what you'd say. But even without telling you, I've been hearing your voice in my head." It's frustrating.

"I think it's your conscience you're hearing. On some level, you know you want more than what Jason can give you. Maybe you feel guilty leaving him behind, since he's had cancer. But he's not your responsibility."

Loud footfalls clamber down the steps, announcing the end of nap time. Will lands with a thud on the landing, and Natalie beams. "I've got a little one who wants Auntie time."

"Go sled?" she asks in her adorable toddler-speak.

I'm not entirely sure there's enough snow to go sledding, but there's no harm in trying.

twenty-nine

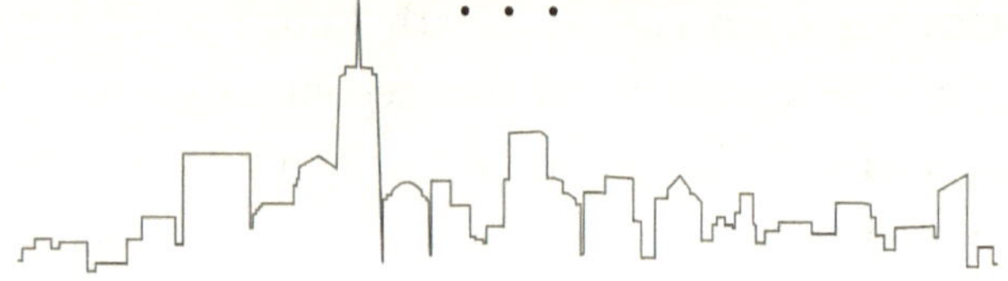

Jason

Dr. Clemmons, or Shannon, crosses her legs, then uncrosses her legs, as she reads my journal entries. When she finishes, she gives me a doctor smile. It's an expression that says she's a professional, and she's going to attempt to make me better. I'm quite familiar with the doctor smile.

"When you wrote these entries, did you feel any emotions?"

I swallow and think back. "No. Not really."

Shannon's manner is thoughtful, reflective. "Can you tell me about how you feel right now?"

"Not good."

The position of her head and the way she nods tells me she wants me to say more.

"To some extent, I feel dead inside. Sometimes it feels hard to breathe. It's not literally hard to breathe, but that's how it feels."

"Do you feel this way all the time?"

I stare at a corner in her room, giving myself time to consider her question. "No. When I'm with Maggie, it's not as intense." She makes things better just by being near me.

"But when you're with her, you still feel this deadness, a sense of suffocation?"

Yes. The pain in the center of my chest never goes away, not completely.

Shannon's waiting for an answer. I tell her, "To some extent, yes."

"Has anyone ever talked to you about survivor's guilt?"

I shake my head. I've never been to a shrink before. Or at least, I've never talked to one. Not like this. But something has to change. Otherwise, I wouldn't have asked her to squeeze me in on a Saturday.

"When I read your journal, it occurs to me to some extent you might be struggling with survivor's guilt. We can explore that. Do you fear your cancer might return?"

"Wouldn't anyone?" I'm sitting in the fortune teller's lair, and she's telling me obvious things like I loved my mother. The doctor smile returns.

"Yes. It's natural. Can you tell me, do you change anything in your life because of that fear?"

I should have Maggie here. "I drink vegetable and herb juice. Some concoction Maggie believes helps improve immunity. And she's careful about selecting every brand of anything in my apartment. Toothpaste, detergent, cleaning supplies. She's always reading about ingredients and switching out what I buy or bringing stuff over."

"She sounds like she cares for you very much, to do all of that. Do you participate too?"

"No. She's been doing it for so long. And I know I should

be more proactive. Do more research. Keep up with advances. But…" I don't like reading about it. Once, I read everything. Every journal, blog, health magazine, top-selling and never-heard-of books. Then Adam died, and it felt like it was a waste of time. All those so-called experts know shit. For the most part, it's a cesspool of groups trying to make money.

"But?" Her question is soft.

"Maggie keeps up with it all."

Shannon glances over her shoulder, at her desk. "Jason, we only have thirty minutes today. But I think there are many things we can work on. I believe we can help with that pain you are feeling."

Wait for it. She's selling something.

"Have you ever heard of EMDR? Or brainspotting?"

"No."

"I'm going to email you some links about them. I've found great success using those techniques, and they don't require that you relive past experiences, which can be quite traumatic. At our next session, we can talk about it and see if it's something you might be interested in trying."

———

Come Monday evening, I'm standing on the sidewalk on Manhattan Avenue, beside Maggie's nondescript apartment entrance. There are four concrete steps up to a glass door with an iron frame and seven iron bars designed to match the low iron fence and gate that defines the front of her building. A small panel of buttons with names scribbled and marked out beside black rectangular buttons lies beside the entrance door. I have a key and could have let myself up to wait for her, but I want to be here when she arrives so I can carry her luggage up the stairs.

Trees line Manhattan Avenue, and as I wait, I notice the color of the leaves is changing. Two trees across the street, near the Hesperus apartment entrance, hold leaves transitioning directly to the crinkly burnt look unhealthy trees get in the fall. Soon, those trees will be barren. But the tree closest to me, on my side of the street, is ablaze in shades of red.

I return my watch to the street, scanning passing cabs for the one Maggie's in. She hasn't responded to any of my texts. She's always busy when she goes home. She and Zoe talk nonstop. I hope that's why she hasn't responded. But nausea has been circulating through me ever since she left. My temperature has remained normal, my glands aren't swollen, and all signs are beginning to point to the nausea being psychological. It could be my gut instincts kicking in, telling me all is not okay with Maggie and me.

I've been an idiot. I've pushed it. Crossed lines repeatedly that should have never been crossed. When the cab pulls up, and she sees me through the rear passenger window, I breathe air through my mouth like a guppy out of water, seeking oxygen.

The corners of her lips barely lift in greeting. I stiffen at her cold response. This isn't Maggie. She pays the cab as I tap the trunk so the cabbie will pop it open.

I come around to greet her. When she exits the back seat, there's a flash of awkwardness, then like a resolved glitch, it's gone. She's wearing her black business pantsuit, and her wavy hair rests in a low, neat bun. It's formal Maggie, but when she hugs me, and I breathe her in, she's familiar. The way my body reacts as I hold her close, you'd think I hadn't seen her in months. My skin tingles, the dead zone in my chest stirs, and that crushing pain rises, forcing me to blink back tears.

"I've missed you." *You have no idea how much.* "How was the trip? The interview?"

She pats my chest a few times and steps to her apartment door. She digs down into her large brown shoulder bag for her keys. I have them on my key ring, in my pocket, so while she rummages in that bottomless pit, I reach around her and unlock the door.

"Thanks."

We make it up the stairs without saying anything. This is not our normal. My nausea elevates. I breathe deeply and swallow back some of the extra saliva pooling in my mouth. We're entering her apartment when it occurs to me she never answered my question.

"Are you taking the job?"

"Sit." She points at her sofa.

I take my normal spot on the right end, and she joins me, shoulders back, sitting prim and proper on the edge with her thighs squeezed tightly together, hands folded in her lap. This is not normal.

"The interview went well. They called me when I was at the airport and offered me the job."

"Maggie, that's great. You're going to take it, right?" She deserves this.

"I am." She's not smiling, and the absence of her smile tells me something isn't right.

"I probably won't be able to move until after spring semester. When do they want you to start?" There's a chance I could swing leaving Columbia after the fall semester, but it's highly doubtful I could do so without burning bridges.

"Jason, what are we doing?"

It becomes harder for me to breathe, and I press two fingers to my wrist. I should go check my temperature. I haven't had a fever, but some viruses don't immediately deliver a fever.

"Jason?" Pressure on my knee brings me back to the room. She squeezes, not comforting—no, in frustration. Shit.

"I'm sorry. I'm not feeling well."

"I can check your temperature." That's good. I nod to tell her that, yes, that's a good idea. "After we talk."

I suppose that's fine. Although, if I'm contagious, I don't want to get her sick. I back up on the cushion, far enough away that her hand returns to her lap.

"Jason, I realized some things this past weekend."

"Yeah?" I'm a little dizzy, so I lean back on the sofa and focus on what she needs to tell me.

"I want a family. I want children. I want a marriage."

"You've known this. That's not new," I say because it's true. One look at Maggie, and it's abundantly clear she's going to be a phenomenal mother one day. She'll be the kind of mom who will have all the neighborhood kids coming over for cookies and hot chocolate.

She breathes in loudly, and her brown irises penetrate me, glassy, full of emotion. "I want those things with you."

I can't breathe. My lungs stop functioning. A numbness spreads across my skin.

"I know you don't want those things with me. I don't fully understand it, because I think we're great together. Maybe it's because you see me as Adam's girlfriend? Maybe you can't get over that?" Her words fly out of her mouth at a rapid pace.

The walls bear down on me. I know I need to say something, but what? The pain in my chest intensifies. It could be a heart attack or some undiagnosed heart issue.

"Don't worry. You'll tell me when you want to. But here's the thing I realized. The thing that is new. I'm almost thirty-two. If you and I live in the same city, I'll fall into old patterns. All my time will be spent with you. I'll never meet someone. I'll never…I don't want you to move to Chicago. This needs to be my break. This needs to be my chance to start something new."

She swipes at her face. Tears mar her cheeks. Nausea curls up the back of my throat, and I rush out of the room, down the hall, and into her bathroom where I hurl the contents of my stomach into her toilet. The only thing I've had today is her juice, so a disgusting green, slimy mess swirls in the porcelain bowl.

"Are you okay?" I hear the tap water running, then it stops. Maggie hands me a warm washcloth and gently caresses my neck. "Let's take that temperature."

There's no fever. She leaves me with my toothbrush after placing a small swab of toothpaste on it.

When I open the bathroom door, her back is to me. Her shoulders quiver, and I hear her sniffling. She's crying.

"I'm okay. Probably just a bug."

"I know." She doesn't turn around.

"I should probably go so I don't get you sick."

She still doesn't turn around.

"Maggie, if you change your mind, I'll move to Chicago in a heartbeat."

"And if you're a good friend, you won't."

thirty

Maggie

"No words are sufficient. I know this, but I do want to tell you how sorry I am for your loss." Mr. Wilcox's fiancée passed away hours ago. When I came in for my volunteer shift at Bellevue, someone pointed him out. He's been sitting on a bench outside of her hospital room, lost. He's not in the area where I volunteer, but I've met him a few times, simply because he's been here so much for the last couple of months.

Mr. Wilcox's shoulders sag. He's in his late twenties, early thirties, tops. Far too young to have this life experience, and I do know what he's going through. Although I wasn't engaged. He's lucky, in a way. Chances are good her family will treat him like a family member, although it's not guaranteed. If I remember correctly, her family is on the west coast. Still, I'm surprised they aren't here. We had known the end was near for quite some time. Maybe they were waiting for hospice before flying out.

The empty hospital bed has a chilling effect, and he reminds me why I'm standing before him when he asks, "You know this? How do you know?"

The words could be confrontational, but they aren't. He's not angry...yet.

I sit down on the green metal bench beside him.

"I lost my boyfriend when I was younger. We weren't engaged, but I loved him. We were in college."

He lifts his eyes and sees me now. A fellow human who doesn't know his exact pain, but a similar pain. A pain close enough that I'm not going to tell him it was god's plan and expect those words to be a balm.

"I'm not religious. I declined to talk to the hospital minister. I don't believe I'm going to see her again." He chokes on the last few words through tears.

"I believe she's not in pain anymore. She's not conscious of her death. Like you, I'm not particularly religious, but I envision death as a deep sleep. Returning to the darkness that we came from, an unawareness similar to the womb. I know that's not comforting to everyone, but it's comforting to me."

"Me too." He wipes his face, sniffles, and gazes at the hospital bed. After an extended silence, he says, "How long does the pain last?"

I get the sense he doesn't expect an answer, but I offer one anyway.

"The stages of grief are individual. It can last years. Many say the second year is harder than the first. But here's what you hold on to. You will always miss her, but as time goes by, functioning without her will get easier. At first, you'll have to remind yourself to breathe. You may find yourself having conversations with her or checking your phone for a text. You may leave her voicemail messages. I actually recommend that last one. I think it can be therapeutic. Or writing her letters. You see, she's still in your heart. She's still a part of you."

He bends down, elbows on his knees, head in his hands.

"The days are going to blend into months, seasons will go by, possibly years. The day will come when it doesn't hurt to remember her. You'll always miss her, but it won't always be painful. You'll find that your memories with her are some of your favorite memories. Eventually, without knowing exactly when, you'll find you're ready to make memories with someone else."

He leans back against the wall, shaking his head, refusing to believe he can go on without her. I understand. He's lost. His pain threshold borders on unbearable.

"I just don't understand how this could happen. She was a good person. She didn't even cuss. It doesn't make sense."

"It doesn't. Unless you think about the chaos of the universe." The fluorescent lights above blind me as I home in on the artificial yellow. He doesn't want to be alone, so I let my theories flow. "There are seven billion people on this Earth. I know many people want to believe there's a predetermined plan for all of them, but that's irrational. I believe Richard Dawkins said it best when he compared life on Earth to the grains of sand on the beach. The chances of anyone of us being on Earth are the same as the chances that we could walk out on a beach and pick up one particular pre-chosen grain of sand."

His red-rimmed eyes stare straight ahead at the opposite wall.

"Once we're here, that DNA mix, the family we're born into, the country we're born in, it's all a crapshoot. When it comes right down to it, we're on a giant rock, hurtling through space. Just like other giant rocks and suns and black holes. The universe is vast, dark, and cold. We found ourselves on Earth. A planet protected by an atmosphere, filled with color. By all accounts, we've stumbled into the heaven of our universe. Right here, right now. That pain you feel, one day, it's gonna help you appreciate each sunrise more."

His lips contort, and he tilts his head. He's not ready to look forward.

"Yes, it sucks. But I meant what I said. She'll remain one of your favorite memories. She'll always be in your heart. You will always have her love. The most important thing to hold on to is that it will get better, and when it does, don't throw it away. She wouldn't want you to. Each day on this planet is a gift. It sounds so cliché, but it's true."

He stares at the empty hospital bed, and I force myself to stop before I spill over into my notions on us all having an exit date. Some people find comfort in the idea that everything, even diseases, are part of an intricate plan. I don't. I don't want to believe some higher power picked a three-year-old to get sick. I don't want to believe some higher power gave my first love cancer.

I spend a lot of time in hospitals. One thing I've noticed is that even those people who say they believe god has his reasons, well, I've noticed they pray. If everything is preordained, why pray? Is the hope this higher power doling out horrible punishments according to his grand plan will change his mind? Grant clemency? No, it's desperation. There's nothing else to be done, so they pray.

"How can you bear to volunteer at a hospital? Marcia, she told me you also volunteer at hospice. How do you do that?" He's not the first person to ask me, but it's unexpected that his thought process would lead him to these questions right now.

"It's comforting to me." I pause then watch him. "Weird, huh?"

"No idea. I should get going." He makes no move to get up.

"Did you live together?"

He nods, and fresh tears flow. I've seen this before. He doesn't want to return to his empty apartment.

He wipes his forearm beneath his nose.

"Her family is flying her home. They're planning everything."

Ah. There's nothing for him to do. He's probably in shock right now too. Even when it's expected, it's surreal when it happens.

I reach out and touch his knee. "Have you scheduled your flight out yet?"

"No."

"Here's what I recommend. Go home, book your flight. Drink water. Get in bed. Sleep. You've been up all night. Sleep. When you wake up, decide on your next action item. Something like pack. Or eat."

He stands, takes one step away, and stops. "Are you happy now?"

It's not the kind of question that should make me smile, but I'm lost in my head, and not only do I smile, but I almost laugh. I hold it in, but barely. "I think I might have gotten lost on the way to happy."

He blinks several times. "Well, I hope you get there."

"I hope we both do."

When I return home to my empty apartment, I flip open the lid to my laptop. I read through the offer letter I received earlier today. Then I draft my acceptance email. I could wait and call in the morning, but I don't want to wait.

thirty-one

Jason

Boats float by on the Hudson. Big ones, little ones, and a singular dragon boat crew. I've spent the entire day sitting on this bench. No energy or desire to do more than sit.

Maggie officially accepted the job.

What I hear, on repeat, are Maggie's words. *I need space.* She doesn't want me to move to Chicago. She doesn't want me around her. She's moving, she won't be here much longer, and she doesn't even want me there.

I don't know how we got here. On some level, I know it's what needs to happen. It's time for her to move on to that next stage of life. She's probably right that it's not going to happen if I'm with her all the time, and she absolutely deserves everything. I want her to have everything. It hurts like a mother, though, because I wish with every part of my being I could be the one to give it to her.

I miss her so fucking much. At this moment, she's two blocks away, but she might as well be in Chicago.

The sun goes down behind the New Jersey skyline, and the temperature drops. The dark brown water transitions to a murky black. Lights reflect off the darkness in patches. An occasional horn sounds in the background, punctuated by a shrill siren or raised voices.

I didn't bring my phone with me out here. There's no point. She hasn't texted or called in days. This, right here… this is my new life. It sucks.

I have no appetite and no desire to eat alone. I'll flip something on until I fall asleep. In the morning, I'll grade papers. I'll let Schlosberger know I won't be making any of the upcoming deadlines. This is a weekend without Maggie. The life I lead now. It's all for Maggie. I love her enough to ensure she gets the best of everything.

When I reach the landing of my apartment building, my super, Scott, is standing in front of my door, and the door is wide open.

"Scott, what's going on?"

Ollie, Sam's younger brother, fills my doorway. "Jason! There you are. What the fuck? Why haven't you returned any of my calls?"

"Returned your…? What the fuck are you doing in my apartment?" I push past him.

"Man, I've been trying to reach you for days. You wouldn't answer your door last night. Or today. I was worried, okay?" He's sheepish, as he should be. What the fuck? I didn't answer because I didn't fucking want to.

The headache I've been nursing all day throbs, and I rub my forehead. I want to be alone.

Ollie stands in front of me, silent.

"Get the fuck out." I grunt out the words, like some sort of injured animal.

"Man. It's not like you to not return my calls. I got scared. Okay?" He reaches for me, and it's too much.

"I'm not an invalid. What the fuck did you think? Get out. Go." I clench my fists to control the anger and all kinds of other emotions flooding me. This is my apartment. My home. My privacy. He has no right.

Boots on my hardwoods echo, and Sam enters the den.

"You too? You're supposed to be in…" I stop. He should be away with his new girlfriend on a weekend I helped him plan, but it doesn't matter. "You know what? I don't even want to know. Both of you, get the fuck out of my apartment. Now."

Holy shit. The room blurs and it's like I can't breathe. My head. My chest. Everything fucking hurts. I storm down the hall and slam the bedroom door, trusting they'll leave me the fuck alone and close the door on their way out. What the hell were they thinking? That I'd off myself?

This sucks. It absolutely sucks. But it's not like I'm entertaining suicide. Like that's an option. People like Adam die when they want to live. I'm not going to kill myself after surviving cancer. After all, I'm the lucky one.

thirty-two

Maggie

"They gave you four weeks' pay when you resigned?" Yara stands in the doorway, gobsmacked. She's working from home today, something she does every Friday and most Mondays.

Flattened cardboard boxes, stacked several inches high, block the narrow path between my bed and the wall. It's day one of packing.

"Crazy, huh? She wasn't mad at all. She told me it's standard when an employee leaves and goes to a competitor." The roll of tape I need to reconstruct the flattened boxes must have rolled underneath the bed, as I can't find it anywhere. I get down on my hands and knees, searching.

"I've never heard of that. I mean, I've heard of people being escorted out of the building when they leave to work for a competitor. But the four weeks' pay, everyone would be jumping to competitors if that was normal. Did you have to do anything?"

"No." I stand, my hunt for tape unsuccessful. "She had me sign some papers and gave me a box to clear out my stuff, but she was super friendly. Happy for me. Offered to be there if I ran into any questions in my director role."

Yara leans against the door frame, both hands wrapped against her oversized coffee mug. "What kind of papers?"

I can't find the roll of tape and want to scream. I circle, surveying the disaster of my room and the crapload of stuff I need to pack.

"Maggie." Yara's stern use of my name brings me back to her.

"Papers. Non-disclosure agreements. Standard stuff when going to a competitor. Although a competitor doesn't feel right. We're all on the same team. Raising money for research to fight cancer and other diseases."

"I agree. It seems crazy."

"It's because McLoughlin is run by a politician. They're all about NDAs."

"So, just like that, you're done with work? Paid leave for the next four weeks?"

I scoot onto the side of my bed. "Yeah. It felt weird, being ushered out so quickly after giving my notice. I worked there for eight years, and poof, it's over. Goodbye, everyone."

In truth, I'm still reeling from it all. A change in job, move to a different city, saying goodbye to my friends. Moving away from Jason. If I think too much about what this means, what it will mean to our friendship, I nearly crumble. I'm broken apart inside. The pain is intense and follows me every-where. I feel it in the morning when I wake, at night when I curl into a ball and will it away. What keeps me moving forward is the knowledge this move is for the best. Jason and me, what's been going on between us, it's not healthy.

This move is a good thing. I'll start my new job in three weeks. Zoe's going into Chicago this week to check out some apartments I found online. If one of them works out, I could be moving by the end of the week, giving me time to get settled in my new city before starting a new job.

"Are they giving you a going-away party?"

"There was no time." We're a small office. Not many people leave, but we do usually bring out cakes. The last time someone left was a few years ago when Mary Elizabeth was on maternity leave and decided she wasn't coming back. So, it was more of a baby shower than a going-away gathering. She still helps out on special events in a freelance capacity.

There's a knock on the door, then the sound of the lock turning carries down the hall.

Yara turns to me with a grin. "One guess who that is."

I leap over the stack of cardboard boxes so I can peer down the hallway just as Jason pushes the door open. One arm is wrapped around a vase of flowers. He must have brought my weekly flower delivery by the office and learned I no longer worked there.

Yara practically shouts down to him, checking her wrist for dramatic effect. "I expected you an hour ago, Longevite."

He glares at her as he shuts the door.

"You didn't give two weeks' notice?"

I step past Yara to retrieve my flowers. "I did."

The flowers tickle my face as I breathe them in. This week, he picked an eclectic mix of fragrant wildflowers from the market. The bunch includes daisies, apple blossoms, honeysuckle, and blue hyacinth. I place them on the kitchen table and admire them. Sadness overwhelms me. These will be the last flowers Jason gives me. An era is coming to an end.

"They said you don't work there anymore?"

"They gave me four weeks' paid leave and wished me luck." His eyes widen. "It sounds confrontational, but it wasn't. Jane was incredibly nice. And it's good. It will give me time to get settled in before work starts. Do you want any coffee? Something to drink?"

"Don't you find it suspicious that she gets upset you shared financial information with me, and then days later you're offered a job in Chicago where Senator McLoughlin lives?"

Yara adds, "They had her sign NDAs."

I frown at her for stirring the pot. She's settled herself down in our big, comfy chair, apparently to observe Jason and me interact. She's fully aware things are not good between the two of us and she should give us some privacy. But that's not Yara. Not by a longshot.

"They gave you four weeks' pay in exchange for signing an NDA?"

"When you say it like that it sounds sketchy."

"It is sketchy, Maggie." He steps forward and uses his height advantage to intimidate.

I'm over this. I skirt away from him and head into the kitchen for a fresh cup of coffee. He follows me.

"Maggie, doesn't this bother you?"

I slam the coffee mug down on the counter.

"Is it so hard to believe my skill set is unique? That someone might want my experience? That I earned this job?" Yes, he might not see much to value in me, but that doesn't mean no one will.

He stares up at the ceiling and waits. He can't stand confrontation. I know this. I show him my back as I pour my coffee.

"It doesn't matter. You're getting out of that company. That's what's important." In a lower voice, almost to himself, he adds, "Moving on."

There's a sadness to him, a melancholy that hits me bone-deep. I ache for him. He's going to have a harder time on his own than I will, and deep down I've always known this. Maybe that's why it's taken me so long to step outside the clutches of our friendship. He's an introvert of the highest order, and it takes time to get to know the considerate, sweet guy he is. Even Yara, who has known him for years, has yet to warm to him, and I tell her all the good things.

I wrap my arms around my friend, and he holds me. We stand together, not letting each other go, even when Yara walks into the kitchen to refresh her coffee.

I close my eyes and burrow against him, memorizing the moment. His subtle Tom's of Maine deodorant mixed with fresh soap scent. I can visualize the all-natural, homemade bar of milky brown I handpicked for him. The fresh, ironed crispness of his shirt, tucked into his thick cotton brown slacks, and those navy blue and orange sneakers. The steady thud of his heart, vibrating through my own.

He tugs at my hair. I lift my head, off his chest, reluctant. I don't want us to end. His lips fall to mine, and I open. He tastes of coffee with a hint of mint toothpaste. Our kiss is slow and tender. Tears coat my cheeks because I know it's goodbye, and I love him with all my soul.

He trails soft kisses over my wet cheeks and dots my forehead with kisses, as I trace the lines of his bicep, holding on as long as I can.

"I'll come see you in Chicago."

"I wish you could see me as yours, and not as Adam's." I breathe out the words I've thought so many times but never said. The words I've silently wished over birthday cakes, and when I've caught a stray eyelash before blowing it out into the cosmos.

"I wish he had lived for you." His response catches me off guard. He pulls away, head down, shoulders caved inward. He looks back, once, right before he closes the door.

thirty-three

Maggie

"What're you doing here? Uh-uh. Back on up and go home. We've had enough of you."

Yara's voice echoes through the dingy metal walls of the U-Haul I rented to drive to Chicago. Zoe flew out, and she's driving back with me. It's gonna be a sister adventure, a road trip for the books.

I crawl over some boxes. I had been checking everything for stability. Since Yara owns most of the furniture in her place, I don't have enough stuff to fill the entire U-Haul, but I have too much stuff to fit in a regular car.

I peer around the side of the van. Jason's back is to me, and Zoe and Yara appear to be telling him exactly what they think. They've been helping me to see he hasn't been my friend, and he hasn't treated me well. Still, he's been my best friend for over ten years. We've always been there for each other. I'm going to miss him. I'm going to miss this era in my life.

"Jason? You came to say goodbye?"

He peers into the van. "There you are."

I side-eye Zoe and Yara, mentally entreating them to give us some space. I have no doubt they had planned on ushering him away without my ever knowing he stopped by.

Yara's girlfriend, Jennifer, loops her arm through Yara's and whispers something in her ear. Zoe stomps her foot and huffs, her outward tells that she's annoyed at the situation.

"I'm gonna go up and check for any more boxes. Fill up our water bottles too. You need anything?" Zoe pointedly asks me, giving me an opportunity to keep her there or to join her.

"I'm good. Thanks."

Zoe ascends the steps to our apartment, and Jennifer nudges Yara forward to follow. I sit down on the back of the U-Haul. It's a bitterly cold day, but the sky is clear, and that's about as much as one can hope for on a November moving day.

Jason shoves his hands into his back pockets and kicks his sneaker up against a flattened soda can, sending it several inches to the curb. A white sedan pulls up to park in the unclaimed parallel parking space behind mine, forcing Jason to step closer to me.

"It was nice of you to stop by."

"Did you think I wouldn't?"

I flick some dirt off my jeans before meeting his dark brown eyes. "Nah. I knew you'd stop by at some point."

"I've been looking at airfare. I can come out this coming weekend and help you unpack. Get your TV set up, hook up anything you need. You might need shelves or something built."

"Thanks for the offer, but I'll have Will to help. My parents are taking care of Natalie, so he's driving in to help unpack. Then he'll drive Zoe home."

"That's this weekend. He won't be there next weekend, right?"

He steps forward, eliminating most of the space between us. I suppress the urge to push him back and work to ignore how my heart rate spikes and hope emerges. There is no reason to hope, and my reaction to this, to my friend standing near me, is exactly why I need to move. We had a good friendship that worked well for us, but somewhere along the way, it stopped working. It became unhealthy. At least from my side, our friendship is no longer a positive in my life. It hurts, and that's a sign I need to let go.

He lifts my chin, forcing me to look at him. "Is it better if I arrive on a Friday or a Saturday?"

"Jason." I reach for his hand, lift it off my face, and hold it on my lap. "I don't know. When are finals? Don't you have a lot to do before the break?"

"Maggie, you'll always be my priority. I can grade on the plane. You know, I was thinking about it, and we can call each other when we're watching TV, and it will be like we're together. We'll just keep the phone on speaker."

"You're a goof." I squeeze his hand, and he intertwines our fingers. "Remember the last time we moved? Our drive from New Hampshire to New York?"

"Yeah, I do. It feels like I should be moving with you to Chicago. Like it should be me and you in the cab of that U-Haul driving away."

I agree. But for obvious reasons, that's not happening. He leans against my legs, his lips inches from mine.

"It's not what you want. You've worked so hard for Columbia. This is where you should be."

"I meant what I said, Maggie. I'd move in a heartbeat if you asked."

"Jason, don't you think we need the time apart? We're in our early thirties and spend all our time with our friend. It's time we develop a real relationship with someone. Both of us. And it's not going to happen with us together all the time. I'm thinking of this as a transition to the next phase of our life."

His thumb passes over my lips, ever so softly. I gather my courage and look up. He gazes with intent, as if memorizing every aspect of me. Then his head dips, and my breath catches, and I plant both palms on his chest and push.

"Jason, what the hell? You tell me you can't be with me as more than a friend, but then you go to kiss me. You are pulling me along, playing with me like a cat toying with a mouse it's going to eat. What am I to you? Entertainment?"

His gaze falls to the ground, and he retreats until the backs of his legs ram up against the white car parked behind him.

"I can't do it, Jason. You have no idea how much it hurts me. I want more. If you wanted more, it would be the two of us in this beat-up piece of junk driving to Chicago. So, don't stand there and make me feel bad with this dejected expression. Don't make me feel guilty. Our issue isn't me. I give you everything." I choke up and pause, batting back the tears welling in my eyes. I have cried enough. "I gave you everything."

"I love you, Maggie. I always will."

I back up onto the curb, needing space. Our normal is for me to tell him I love him. I always say it back. But today, I won't.

Of course, I do. I do love him. But today is the day when saying it back won't help either of us. Kissing him back will hurt me. I don't have any idea what the fuck it does to him.

He steps up to me and wraps his arms around me, pulling me up next to him, bending down as if he's going to kiss me again, and it's the absolute last straw. I push my hands against him, once more, because that's us. We do everything on repeat. But this is the end. This is when this cycle ends. I take a step backward.

"Jason, I meant what I said. I need space. Don't come visit me in Chicago. Do you understand?"

I wait for his visual recognition, for his silent agreement. His shoulders are rounded, his hands shoved in his front pockets, and he has the saddest expression I've ever seen on him. It's possible it's the light from the overcast day, but his eyes are so dark I can't delineate the pupil, and glassy, as if he might cry.

I've never seen him cry, and I can't bear seeing it today. So, I spin and charge up the stairs to my apartment entrance, leaving him behind.

thirty-four

Jason

"On a scale of one to ten, where would you say your pain level is today?"

Shannon asks me the question, clueless as to how many times I've been asked that by medical professionals.

"Ten." Things can't get worse.

I'm staring at a clump of something on her carpet. I don't care enough to see her reaction. I'm not trying to get a reaction. I want the pain to end, and she's the last resort. I don't actually expect she can help, but when you have no other options, and the pain is bad enough, you try anything.

"How long has the pain level been at a ten?"

"Since Maggie left."

"Maggie, your best friend?"

I nod.

"What do you mean by left?"

"She moved to Chicago."

"Do you want to talk about it?"

"No."

"Okay. Did you get a chance to read the material I sent you? About brainspotting? And EMDR?"

I nod. Brainspotting is an advanced brain-body therapy that focuses on identifying, processing, and releasing imbalances, trauma, and residual emotional stress. It is based on the premise that "where you look affects how you feel." They believe eye positions correlate with unconscious, emotional experiences. It seems crack-pottish, but when desperate, it's worth a try. It can't hurt. A shrink and meds are an option, but I've already fried my brain. I'd rather avoid dousing it with more chemicals.

This woman sitting in front of me comes highly recommended by Janet, Sam's assistant. She has vast resources to research medical professionals, and she swears Shannon, Dr. Clemmons, knows her shit.

"I've found brainspotting can be helpful, especially when past experiences may be too painful to share or relive."

I nod. I heard it all on the video she sent over with the information. They use it a lot on PTSD patients. Trauma. I haven't had trauma, but again, it can't hurt.

Shannon hands me a headset connected to an outdated iPod. I slip it on my head and resume staring at my favorite spot on the floor.

"I want you to follow this with your eyes."

She's holding out a thin, expandable metal rod with a white cloth rounded end. She's holding it directly in front of her face. The pain in my chest intensifies, and I want to look away, but I force myself to focus on the white swath. The sounds of waves crashing on a beach filter through the headset.

Slowly, Shannon moves the rod to the left. "I want you to pay attention to the pain in your chest. I want to find a location where you feel the tightness intensify."

A little voice that sounds a lot like Adam says, "What a crock of shit." But I have nothing to lose, so I trail the rod.

As the rod moves farther away, my chest lightens. It's noticeably easier to breathe. The crushing pain is still present, but as she returns the rod to the front of her face, it tightens again, and I shake my head and point, directing her to return it to the side.

She does so, this time lifting the rod higher to the right quadrant. I hold out my hand, telling her she's found a good place.

"Now what?"

"Focus on the end of the rod."

She doesn't provide any other instructions. The waves crashing sound louder, and a drumbeat joins in.

I stare at the white tip. Milky white blurs my peripheral vision. I blink to maintain focus. The sound transitions to rain and thunder.

Moments from my past, visuals frozen in time, flip by.

The first is the memory of a photograph from my baby book. It's me, with a cone birthday cap strapped on, blowing out candles on a white birthday cake with yellow dots around the perimeter.

The second is Dad, pushing my bicycle down the street. I remember the day. The image is of my back, a perspective I wouldn't have had unless somewhere there's a photo.

Then my mother, sitting beside me in the emergency room, as I pick out the color for my cast.

The white around my periphery intensifies, and I blink, breathing deeply. The pain crushes me, and I glance back to my carpet spot for relief. Then I return my focus to the dot.

Snapshots of ski vacations over the years flit through. No surprise. My parents' house was covered with these shots. The photos where you're positioned by a photographer on a picturesque mountain spot with your group, and the resort logo is emblazoned in the bottom right-hand corner. Image after image flashes by. At first, it's me and my parents, then we're joined by the Dukes.

Then images of the day. The images I relive in my nightmares. I keep staring. The pain slices and hurts. My parents, in their caskets. The music transitions to an orchestra, and the constant drum keeps pace. I open my mouth to breathe in, gasping.

All I see is the dot. Waves crash through the headset. I pull the headset off. She didn't say how long, but I'm done.

I hand the headset to her.

"Are you done?"

I nod.

"Are you ready for me to put this away?"

"Yes." She smiles her doctor smile.

"How was that?"

"Intense."

"How do you feel now?"

I close my eyelids and rest my head against the back of the couch, taking stock. The pain in my chest, the suffocating sensation, it's all there. But it's slightly better.

"A little better."

"What would you say your pain threshold is at now? On a scale of one to ten?"

"Eight. Maybe nine."

A relieved expression flashes before she says, "That's good. Do you want to tell me about your experience?"

"It was like I saw photographs. From the past."

"From one specific period of time?"

I shift back on the uncomfortable couch, cross my ankle over my thigh, and resume staring at my spot on the carpet as I think about what I saw.

"Mostly from my childhood. My parents."

"You don't mention your parents in your journal. What happened to them?"

I tilt my head back until it hits the wall, then rub my hand across my face. What the…? I pull my hand back. It's wet. I've been crying. I don't cry.

I grind my teeth. Close my eyes. "They died in an avalanche."

"Were you with them?"

"No." I shake my head, this time fully conscious of the tears streaming. "I should have been."

"Why do you say that?"

"They'd still be alive. If I had gone with them, they wouldn't have been where they were at the time of the avalanche. They would have arrived at the spot a few minutes later, maybe five or ten minutes later, and the avalanche would have been over, and they would be alive."

"Jason, it's not your fault your parents died."

"Yes. It is. I wanted to go skiing with my friends. They wanted me to spend the last day of our trip with them. And I didn't. If I had just gone with them."

Shannon moves to sit beside me on the sofa. She's the first person I've ever said this to. On some level, I know I sound illogical. Even so, it's true. Therefore, not irrational.

"It's not your fault."

I break down, crying like a child.

"It's not your fault."

I cry harder.

"It's not your fault."

I cry. She keeps repeating those four words. "It's not your fault."

thirty-five

Jason

"You know, the problem with this despondent thing you've got going on is I don't know if I should be concerned or not." Sam sets the thick pint glass down on the wooden table with a thud. He forced me to come out for drinks with him. Olivia is home studying. They moved in together over six months ago. Right around the time Maggie moved to Chicago.

I respond by sipping my lukewarm beer. Sam and I are close enough that if I don't feel like talking, he can deal with it.

"All right. Let me try a different angle. Mom...you remember her, right?"

Patti Duke's concerned. She's been my surrogate mom since my parents passed. She'd probably be blowing up my phone, except she's careful with how she expresses her concern. When I was younger and didn't handle things well,

I lost control. Let her have it when she was suffocating me with her worry and pity. Now she employs Sam as her concern funnel.

"It's not cancer." We stare at each other. I cave. "I'll call her."

"She'd appreciate it. She loves you, you know. Dad does too. We all do."

"I know. I love you guys too." He stares me down. I exhale loudly so he knows I don't appreciate the inquisition. Then guilt kicks in. It won't kill me to let him in. "It's been hard since Maggie left. I miss her." Missing her is an enormous understatement, but it's Sam I'm talking to.

"You guys were kind of inseparable. I can see how it would be an adjustment."

"You have no idea. I go to text her to ask what she wants to order for dinner, then remember she's not here. I find myself walking to her apartment all the time and catch myself when I'm about a block away. It's like I'm on autopilot. It's like…have you ever heard that when someone loses a limb, they have phantom pains?"

He nods.

"It's like that. I expect her to still be here, the same way I'd expect my leg to still be there if it was amputated."

Sam's index finger traces the condensation on the side of his glass, pensive.

"Do you think she's seeing anyone?" It's a question I keep asking myself, so I ask out loud.

"How would I know?"

"You wouldn't. I'm just…we've never gone this long without talking. I've lost my best friend. It sucks."

His face contorts.

"What?" I ask.

"It's good to hear you talk about what's going on. We all had theories, but never mind. As far as Maggie goes..." He spreads his hand out flat on the table. "Even if she is dating someone, you can still be friends. Over the years, you've both dated other people. It got awkward. You never said much, but I could tell things were tense. But your friendship survived."

"It got awkward?"

"I mean, from the outside looking in. Remember the time she backed out last minute from Mom's birthday brunch in the city?"

"She had something come up with work."

"It was when you were dating some girl. Stacy, maybe?"

"Maybe Sara. It was an S. It doesn't matter...what are you saying?"

"She didn't come around as much if you were dating, but then your friendship picked back up. And remember when she was dating Glen?"

"That guy was such a tool." Just remembering that guy makes my shoulder muscles tense, which is saying something because I'm not exactly happy-go-lucky these days.

"You spent more time with me. And they were together for, like, a year."

"A long damn time," I remember. He and I did not like each other.

"What does it matter if she's dating someone now?"

"It doesn't. But I think not knowing makes her move away suck even more. I fucked up. We crossed the friendship line. She wanted space. How do I know when she's had enough space? It's been months." I've been debating reaching out to Maggie and planning a visit. We didn't see each other over Christmas break. She wanted space, and I've given it to her in spades.

"Reach out and ask."

I'd already bought plane tickets to visit her when she told me not to come. Had been planning to surprise her and be there all week helping her get situated. Figured we could paint her apartment, and I could help her find furniture. Help her find a car and negotiate the price for her since she hates negotiating. But standing by her moving van, she made it clear she didn't want me there, so I canceled that trip. She gave me no choice.

"Why don't you want to date Maggie? I know Ollie and I joke about it, but I really thought you'd end up with her."

I chew on my thumbnail as I consider my answer. "The short answer? I was just lost in my head."

"You're not now?"

"I don't know. I'll probably always be a little fucked up." It's the truth. Sam taps his glass against mine.

"You're not fucked up. You've just been through a lot."

"No, I blew it. Maggie's the best thing ever, and I kept her at arm's length." For her—I did it for her. But I didn't do it well. I hurt her.

"Well, maybe you blew your chance of a relationship with her. But you don't walk away from a friendship like yours. Reach out."

I did call her Christmas morning. I've spent many Christmas mornings at her parent's' home, so I could envision everything on her end. The Christmas tree with their family decorations, many of them featuring a photo and the year, the holiday moose collection her Mom scatters throughout the den, and the constant holiday music playing through Alexa.

When she answered the phone, it was the first time we'd spoken since she moved. Our conversation was filled with awkward silence. We didn't have anything to talk about, really. I mean, I had a million things to ask her, but she gave clipped answers. When her Mom called her away for breakfast, we both wished each other a Merry Christmas. I told her I loved her because I do. There was a pause, and I held my breath. I half expected her to hang up. But she didn't. She said it back.

No matter what happens in our lives, or how we evolve, we'll always love each other. Deep down, I know this. This separation period she's asked for, it's hard. Bloodcurdling hard. I miss her. I miss talking to her. I miss having her in my life. I miss sharing life with her.

A part of me hopes she's found someone else. A great guy who will take care of her, have kids with her, and be her partner. She deserves it. That's the rational part. I've been told I have an extraordinarily high IQ, and this is the part I let lead me through life. I love her, and I want the best for her, and I know I'm not the best that's out there.

Then there's this emotional side of me. This side isn't rational. It resides with all the pain Shannon has been working on releasing in our weekly whacked-out staring sessions.

When I think of Maggie with someone else, the emotional side gets knifed repeatedly. The sharp pain cuts through and makes it hard for me to do anything. I sit on the sofa, still. It's my new nighttime routine. I often skip dinner, and I'm not hungry in the morning.

I have no energy, but I have been forcing myself to go on runs. Short runs, maybe one or three miles, but I force myself out the door, hoping the endorphins will kick in. Hoping I'll feel better.

Sam still reaches out regularly, as does Ollie. I answer the phone and respond to texts often enough they don't pound on my door. I never miss class or an office time. I function. But at the same time, I wonder why I try. What exactly am I living for?

When those thoughts invade, guilt rushes in. Adam would have so much to live for. He'd give anything to be in my shoes. I hate myself for not doing more with what I have. I got to live, and yet I'm not happy. It's like I'm broken or something is wrong with me.

"Hey, where'd you go?" His foot taps mine below the table.

"Thinking." I clink my glass to his. "Thanks for being a good friend."

The next day, when I push open Shannon's office door, I want to talk. It's not that I mind the brainspotting sessions. I don't. They do make me feel better. Often, I'm tired and sleep after them. I sleep better for the next couple of days. But I need to talk to someone. Maggie isn't here, and it's not like this therapist I'm paying can replace her, but I need to talk through these circles.

She's helping with my overall pain. I don't dream about the day on the slopes anymore. If I talk to her, and we do more brainspotting sessions, it's possible I can find my way out of this funk.

I set my journal down on the coffee table. She's typing at the computer but says hello. I don't know why I bring the journal, but she still asks me questions and has me write something each week, even though she doesn't always read it.

"How are you doing, Jason?" She steps away from the computer and joins me in the sitting area of her office.

"Good." It's an automatic response. I have no idea why I say that to everyone who asks. It's so rarely true.

She reaches for the headset, which sits in a basket by the couch.

"I was wondering if we could talk today, instead of doing the…" I point at the headset. I hate that word, brainspotting. "The EMDR thing."

"Certainly." She sets it back down into the basket. "What's going on?"

I rub my forehead and stare at the corner of the room. I didn't plan what to say or how to begin.

"Would you like to write it down?"

"No." I press my eyelids shut and squeeze the top portion of my nose. *I can do this.* "The stuff we've been doing has helped, but at times, the pain…it hits me hard."

"When does this happen?"

I lean back on the couch and smack my skull against her wall. I rub the back of my head, then more slowly rest against the wall and close my eyes, preferring not to see.

"It happens when I think of Maggie with someone else. It hurts. I need to find a way for it to not hurt."

"Jason, we haven't really talked about Maggie. I know from your journals she's important to you. Is she dating someone?"

"Probably."

"Jason…did you and Maggie ever move beyond friendship, into a dating relationship?"

"No."

"Why is that, do you think?"

"It wouldn't be fair to her. I want more for her."

"I'm not sure I understand. Can you explain that to me?"

I shift forward, elbows to my knees, forehead resting on my palms.

"She wants a life with children, and one day grandchildren."

"That's a common desire. Not everyone wants those things. Do you not want those things?"

"No, I'd love to have those things…with Maggie. But that's not in the cards for me."

"I'm not sure I'm following. It sounded like Maggie wanted more than friendship with you."

"She does."

"Right now, it sounds like you're saying you want a relationship with her too. A commitment with her and a life with her."

I lift my head. Shannon seems genuinely mystified, and that annoys me. It's not rocket science. "I had cancer. It could come back. I watched her beside Adam's grave. You read about it in my journal. She deserves a healthy partner. Not someone she's going to have to bury."

Shannon shifts in her chair and crosses her leg with that doctor smile plastered on her face, only there might be a hint of amusement. Maybe. It's gone in a flash.

"Jason, the last time I asked, you were NED. In remission."

"Yes." It's come back before. It can come back again. Or a different form of cancer. Something worse.

"Jason, do you often find yourself with a need to control?"

I stare off into my corner.

"Let me ask a different question. When things don't go how you want them to, do you believe you are responsible?"

"What?"

"Think about your parents. You told me you believe you could have prevented their deaths."

"I could have. If I had just…" I stop. I know she believes it's not my fault. I do too, on some level. I couldn't have known what would happen that day. Skiing with my friends, doing runs my mom wouldn't do, it was an understandable choice.

Shannon waits.

I swallow. "You're right. It's not my fault."

"Do you believe you're responsible for Adam's death? Has that ever crossed your mind?"

"Not responsible. He had cancer. But…it would've been better if it had been me."

"I saw a reference to that in your journal. Do you remember what we call that?"

I shake my head while staring in my corner.

"Survivor's guilt." She likes that concept.

"Okay. What does that have to do with Maggie?"

"I suspect it might be part of the reason you haven't let your relationship with her grow."

"The reasons I think it should've been me who died is he had parents who mourned him. And he had Maggie. His death tore her up. If you could've seen it, you'd understand."

"I read some about it in your journal. If I understand correctly, and I don't want to put words in your mouth, you believe you can prevent Maggie from future heartache by not being with her."

"Yes."

"That's trying to control the future." She pauses, and silence fills the room. "No one can control the future."

"I know that."

"Then you must realize Maggie's future husband could die prematurely, even if it's not you."

"Yes, but it's statistics. It's more likely to happen if it's me. I want her to have the best possible chance."

"Is Maggie dating someone now?"

"I don't know. She asked for space."

"Space for what?"

"Space from us. So she can find someone else."

"Jason, if you could have a guarantee that you could live a full life, would you want to be with Maggie?"

"Yes."

"That's the only thing that's holding you back?"

"Yes." The picture on my dresser of Adam with his arms around her comes to mind. "I mean, her being Adam's girlfriend complicates it, but yes, if I could get a written guarantee, I'd be with her." No question.

"You do know there's no guarantee for anyone, right? Ever?"

"That's why I'm not with her," I snap.

"No, Jason, I'm telling you that no matter who she's with, there's no guarantee."

She doesn't get it. She doesn't understand my risks are higher.

"There's no guarantee for anyone." Shannon likes to repeat herself.

"Can you make it so the idea of Maggie being with someone else doesn't hurt so much?"

She smiles. "With time, it won't hurt so much. But it sounds like you love her."

"Of course I love her. That's never been the question."

"Then maybe we can work on some of the control issues so you can be with her?"

"I don't have …" Control isn't the right word. "Why don't we do a brainspotting session?"

She smiles, but this time she also looks like she wants to laugh. None of this is funny.

She straightens in her chair then reaches for the headset. "Okay. But in your journal this week, can you do something for me? Can you write about what you see your life like if you were to allow yourself a relationship with Maggie?"

When I close Shannon's office door and exit the building onto the street, I do something I haven't done in months. Words from one of Maggie's favorite chick flicks come to mind. The whole scariest thing about distance bit. Maybe she misses me, but maybe she's forgotten. Moved on. Shelved me in the "old friend I used to know" category.

Me
Hi. Checking in. How's Chicago?

I slip the phone into my pocket and have crossed two blocks when the vibrations let me know I've received a text.

Maggie
Hey, you! Things are good. Love my new job.
How're things there?

I step to the side of a deli to respond.

Me
I'm still seeing a therapist.

Maggie
Is it helping?

Me
Yes and no. Can I call you? Or do you still need space?

I make it all the way home before she responds.

Maggie
Sure. I'm an hour behind you. I'll call you when I get home.

thirty-six

Maggie

"There, that should do it. It's all hooked up. Want to hand me the remote?" Xander slides a screwdriver into the back pocket of his well-worn jeans and reaches his arm out.

I reluctantly pass him the remote. It's not that I don't see a reason to have a television. I do. After Xander's incessant prodding, I finally broke down and went out and bought one. He told me he'd install it and get it set up. I'm not paying for cable, so he's helping me with all the apps I'll need to download shows through Netflix, Apple, or whatever he recommends.

It's a transition to a new chapter in my life. For over ten years, Jason was my sofa partner. Now everything's in place for me to find a new TV companion.

I've been making excuses. Keeping things at the friend level with my neighbor on the floor below. Zoe says I'm nuts. He is hot as sin in a boy band kind of way. His real name is

Alexander, but he goes by Xander and has this dark curly hair he keeps tied back in a man bun. Tattoos peek below his sleeves when he wears t-shirts. His irises are almost violet. A bizarre color that had me wondering if he wears colored contacts for the first few weeks I knew him. It's still a possibility. I don't know him well enough to ask, but I haven't detected the telltale circular disc yet.

There's a knock on the door, and I spring to get it, practically bouncing on the way, as I have an idea who might be showing up early.

I love my walk-up apartment, but it's not exactly difficult to slip in without buzzing. Half the time, the door is propped open because some of the downstairs tenants love to smoke cigarettes on the stoop. Plus, it's early summer in Chicago, and there's a general feeling every door and window should be open.

I crack the door then swing it wide.

"Jason."

It feels like years have passed since I last saw him, even though it's only been months. He reached out recently. A couple of weeks ago, he said he'd be in town and asked if he could stop by to visit.

To visit. My best friend asking if he can stop by to visit. Times have changed.

We stand in the doorway, holding each other tight. My feet leave the floor as he lifts me, and I breathe in his soap scent. I didn't buy him the soap I smell. It's not even what I would pick. There's a hint of lemon.

Tears sting, forcing me to blink several times. I've missed this moody ginger so freaking much. No part of me wants to let go, but the television playing in the background reminds me I have company.

"So good to see you," I whisper against Jason's neck. Then, in a louder voice as I break the hug and return to the ground, "Let me introduce you to Xander."

Xander steps around the couch, his hand extended. "Good to meet you, man. She's talked a lot about you. I'm Xander."

Shock crosses Jason's features, but he recovers quickly. "Hi. I'm Jason."

Xander chuckles and points around my den. "Yeah, I know. Not hard to pick you out."

I'm a candid photo lover. Framed photos decorate any available surface. Some line the mantel, some decorate a small table sitting between two windows, some line the narrow table behind my sofa. Jason's in almost all the photos. There is clear photographic evidence almost everywhere he's been an important part of my life.

Jason steps inside and swivels, taking in my new apartment. It's a much better space than my New York pad. This job pays significantly more, plus the cost of living is so much better in Chicago. The walls are painted white, and given the abundance of sun streaming in through the open windows, the whole place feels bright and airy. I've been hitting thrift stores, and all the wooden pieces are finds I've painted in shades of navy. My Jennifer Convertible sofa is my one brand new piece of furniture, and I chose white. Bursts of happy colors pop against the white in the form of throw pillows and large abstract paintings.

My old pad with Yara was fine, in a post-college with roommate sort of way, a hippie chick transitioning to thirty-something kind of apartment. But this place, it's all me. I love it.

"This place looks like you."

"Thanks." I beam up at him, loving how well he knows me.

"What brings you into town?" Xander asks. His arms are crossed, and he rocks back on his feet.

We're all standing in a cluster right in front of the door. The sound of the television drones on, and the noise grates my nerves.

I reach for the remote Xander's holding as Jason responds, "Business."

The TV clicks off at a touch of the button.

"Thank you so much for setting this up," I tell Xander.

"Do you want me to take you through it all? I need to add Netflix."

"I'll deal with it later." The last thing I want is to mess with the TV right now. Setting up accounts. He has the Apple TV working. That's plenty. I've actually enjoyed being TV free. Listening to music, reading, painting furniture. I haven't missed the TV at all. It's been a source of contention between Xander and me.

"Are you thirsty?" I ask Jason. "Can I get you anything? When did you get in?" I haven't seen this guy in ages, and we're huddled by the door talking about a glass screen over the mantel.

"My flight got in a little early." He seems apologetic.

I take off toward my kitchen. He's been on an airplane and in the crowded airport.

"You can wash your hands at the sink if you want," I tell him as I pour a glass of veggie juice for him. I restocked since he was coming into town.

He steps past me to the sink. On the windowsill behind the sink are three framed photos. One is of Yara and Jason sitting on the beat-up futon in our old apartment. A nothing moment but a cute picture. Another is after a Team-in-Training event. It's a group shot, and Jason didn't compete, but he's wearing a team t-shirt, and down by his legs you can read his poster that says "Run Maggie Run!" The third photo is one of my favorites of him. It makes me laugh every time. It's his Halloween costume from our senior year when he dressed up like a 1970s basketball player, complete with short shorts and tall socks. This place is all mine to decorate. It's filled with the things that make me happy.

Xander calls from the hall. My kitchen opens into the den, so I can see him. "I'm gonna head on down and let you guys get in a good visit. Is seven p.m. still good to pick you up?"

"Yep. That works. I can come down to you. It's on the way." I smile and force a laugh to bring life to my sort-of joke. His place is on the way out of the building.

"Not a chance. I'll be knocking at seven." He holds out a fist to Jason for a fist bump, a signature Xander move. "Nice to meet ya. Hope we connect again before you head back."

Jason holds out a stiff arm, and in slow motion the two men's fists touch.

I hunt in the refrigerator to find something to drink while Jason and I catch up. The juice I poured Jason is an easy option, but I have an urge for a beer. Maybe it's the blue sky outside or the Saturday summer feeling. "You want a beer?"

"Sure." He chugs down the juice and sets the empty glass on the counter as I set about pulling two brown glass bottles out and popping the top.

"So, are you and Xander..." He lets the question linger as he washes his hands at the sink.

"No," pops out as my answer, but I don't want to give the

wrong impression either. I set his beer beside the sink. "He's my neighbor. Lives one floor down. We're going out on a date tonight." Guilt lances through me. The emotion annoys me because I have nothing to feel guilty about.

I grab my beer and charge into the living area. Jason follows me. He slides a small black backpack off his shoulder and lays it on the wooden coffee table before sitting down.

"All this stuff is new." He angles his beer to my coffee table. "And white cushions. Mags. That's ballsy."

"Well, it's just me. I don't have a guy to worry about spilling Chinese or leaving pizza crust crumbs all over it." I regret saying it the moment my response falls out of my mouth and exhale louder than normal. "So, tell me why you're here. What business does Columbia University have in Chicago?"

In a way, I'd hoped he was coming to see me. But he never asked if he could stay with me, and it never felt like a good time to ask him why he was coming, so I didn't. His reasons don't matter. It's good to see him.

"I'm interviewing at The University of Chicago on Monday."

"You might move here?" He was well on his way to a full professor role at Columbia, an Ivy League college. That doesn't make sense.

He shrugs. *No big deal*, he communicates through his silent body language I know so well. There's got to be more to it. I open my mouth and lean forward, my body language telling him to tell me more.

He doesn't say anything, but instead unzips his backpack and pulls out a Mead notebook, the kind that looks like someone ran a stripe of white tape on the side in lieu of binding with a spiral. He places the notebook before me on the coffee table.

"What's this?"

He lifts his shoulders. His dark eyes are pensive, with a steady focus on the notebook. "My therapist had me answer questions in it."

I angle my head and squint, another gesture he's familiar with that tells him to explain.

"The therapist I told you about. Dr. Clemmons. Shannon. When I first started seeing her, it was hard for me to talk. So, I put a lot of stuff in there. Some stuff I want to share with you, and talking about it on the phone didn't feel right."

"Now? You want me to read it now?" I stare at the notebook, reluctant to touch it.

"Why not? Not sure there will be a better day. You were planning on spending the afternoon with me anyway, right?"

I pull the notebook onto my lap as he lifts his beer and takes a long swallow. Flipping through, I see it's all in his handwriting in black or blue pen. His handwriting has sharp edges, controlled, each letter an identical size. I've often said he could sell it as his own font. Easy to read with an edge.

The first page is titled "The Day We Met." I slide my beer onto the coffee table then pull my legs underneath me. It's about the day he and I first met when I went with Adam and his parents to an oncology appointment our freshman year. He noticed me that day. I had no idea. I remember that day too. I remember how alone he seemed. And when I realized he was a patient, I remember hoping he wasn't too sick. I drag my finger over the words, *"if she's here for cancer, please let her kind be totally beatable."*

The next titled page reads "Support Group Day." I find this fascinating. I always wondered why the two of them made jokes about support groups. Why the two of them were so anti-therapy. I never pushed Adam to explain. And later, when I tried to push Jason, he'd give one of his non-answers. His reaction to Howard, the older man crying, is insightful. Human beings all mourn, but we react to it so differently. I'm not at all surprised that at nineteen Jason wasn't comfortable. I've met grown adults, men and women, who couldn't handle raw emotion from others, especially strangers. Some people can, and some people can't.

The next titled page reads "The Day We All Met." It's about the day we all met on the lawn in front of the library. He thought I was beautiful. I finger the letters on the page. *When I'm lying on my deathbed, I'm going to close my eyes and remember how she looked that day.*

All these years. His words aren't incredibly descriptive, but reading them is like flipping the pages in a photobook. Only it's from his perspective. He writes that he felt sucker-punched when I kissed Adam. That's an accurate description of how I feel at this moment. I pause on the last line of this section, *They were without a doubt my two closest friends. Adam and Maggie.*

"The Days at Hospice" sends my tear ducts into overdrive. I let the tears fall, swiping them away with the flat of my palm. He gets up and returns to the sofa with a tissue box. As I read, my perspective on these moments strikes full force. The shock. That someone so young, one of *my* friends, might die. The helplessness. My first personal experience with death.

Adam did tell me to take care of Maggie. To look out for her. "She's a good one." He got that part wrong, though. She's the best.

I'm not surprised Adam told Jason to take care of me. And I'm not surprised Jason was looking out for me, even back then. We look out for each other. That's what we do. We've been doing it a long time.

Jason's description of "The Funeral" tugs at long-buried emotions. I had no idea he was watching me. There were many things I said that day to Adam when I said goodbye to my first love. Over time, I came to realize Adam and I had a young love. I had been angry and hurt he hadn't been honest with me about his diagnosis.

When we drove cross-country that summer, I thought cancer was behind him. As we approached California, there were moments when he'd grow quiet, contemplative. In retrospect, there were signs throughout the trip a dark cloud loomed overhead. But, like they say, hindsight is twenty-twenty. At the time, I had no idea.

He grew increasingly somber the closer we got to California. I fancied it was because we'd be apart for the second half of the summer. I suspected maybe he didn't get along with his family, or there was some other reason he dreaded returning home. Now I know the real reasons. And he probably wasn't feeling good. He probably struggled to some degree to hide his physical symptoms.

When we drove into his parents' driveway, his mother held him tight, and tears streamed down her cheeks. At the time, it struck me as odd. Figured she must be the emotional sort and had missed her son.

The two of them argued in the kitchen over where I would sleep. I stood outside in the hall, mortified. I didn't expect to sleep with him in his parents' home and didn't understand why he made such a big deal about it. In the end, I slept in the guest room. The tension in the house was so thick, I couldn't wait to leave for the airport the next day to return home to my family. Jason knows none of that. I've never shared it with him. But it's clear he picked up on the tension; he simply didn't understand it.

I hover over his words *It should have been me*. Oh, Jason. That's not our guilt to carry. We are not gods.

By the time I reach "New Year's Day," my tears have dried. I remember the dress. He's wrong, though. I wasn't sad about going out that night. I only wanted to spend time with him, and I didn't care where we were.

I couldn't do a journal like this. I don't know what day I fell in love with him. I know I love all the little things about him. But when did I transition from loving him to being in love with him? I have no idea.

I know we have a connection. I visualize it as a beam of light flowing between the two of us, connecting us. Even during this time when we've been apart, when I put distance between us for my own good, I could close my eyes, find my center, and feel the bond. Searching for the sensation to know I still had the connection. It's still there. I've never lost it. Silly thing, I know. All in my head. But I swear it's there.

I turn the page. "The Day It Returned." I remember that day. His plan to keep me in the dark. My best friend. Everything in here confirms one of my latent suspicions. He held me at arm's length out of fear he'd get sick again. His attempt to protect me.

I flip through. He talks about a night we stayed in. I don't remember this night, but it describes so many of our nights. What hits me, though, is for years when I struggled, wanting more but respecting that he saw me as a friend, he wanted more too. Only he held me out like a china doll that needed protecting, not trusting me to make my own decisions and take my own risks.

The journal takes a turn. Dates line the top of the page.

He records sensations he felt during his therapy. Thoughts he had. Session after session after session. Written almost more as dream sequences, and they don't make as much sense. He flips pages forward to arrive at the last page.

I gaze into his dark brown irises, silently questioning.

"Those are pages from the therapy sessions I had. It'll sound like hocus-pocus when I tell you about it. You can read it later if you want." He taps the last page. "But read this now."

The Love of My Life

Maggie. Obviously, it's Maggie. It's always been her.

I love everything about her. Her smile. The warmth in her golden-brown eyes. How her hair always has a slightly undone feel, as if she didn't brush it recently. I love that I know she probably hasn't brushed it recently. I fell in love with her in college when she was lanky. I loved her as she became more athletic, and as her curves have filled out over the years.

When I look at her, it's as if a day hasn't passed since freshman year. I'm shocked when I compare photos and realize that, yes, we both looked younger back then. Because when I look at her, I could swear she hasn't changed. I see so much more.

I see all the little things. Twelve years' worth of vegetable juice. Rubber gloves and face masks when she didn't want me to be alone but didn't want to risk getting me sick. A hundred different soup recipes, all created with the hope of finding yet another nutritious, immunity building food. Her kindness. Her heart. It's overwhelming what a good person she is. Only the kindest of souls has the strength to be there for those who are facing death or have lost a loved one. And she does it in her free time.

She's done more to fight cancer than I have. And I'm the one who had cancer. I still fight cancer. Every day.

The way I battle cancer, though, isn't how some might expect. Yes, I fear it will return. But what I fear most is the hurt it will inflict on those I love. It can take me. For years, I wished it had taken me and not Adam. It's not my fault things worked out the way they did. Accepting it's not my fault has not been easy. Or, I should say, accepting I cannot control it has been damn near impossible.

What I want for the love of my life is to give her more than I have to give. I want her to grow old with her husband and happy children. I want her to have a lifetime of laughter. Maggie has the most amazing laugh. I recorded it one time. A couple of times, actually, without her knowing. I play those recordings. When I need to lessen the pain. When I need to remember her. When I want to feel happy.

I know she will find someone other than me. Someone who can give her all those things. But I need her to know I have always loved her and will always love her.

The risks of being with me are great. My cancer could return. My immune system is compromised. Something else could come along. I'm a professor. There's a great chance if I'm alive decades from now, I'll wear sweater cardigans and orthotic shoes. No, scratch that. I'll never give up my sneakers. Still, it's not a bright outlook.

But the biggest mistake I ever made was making the decision for her.

You asked me to tell you what my life would be like if she and I were together. If I were healthy, and I could give her everything.

It would be perfect. That's what my life would be like. I mean,

I'm sure I'd get on her nerves at times. And she'd make me go out when I want to stay in. We'd have kids and a dog. She'd be the most loving mom in the world. And I would be grateful every single day.

To hold her, for her to be mine, that's a dream. It might sound mundane to some, but when I look back on my life, my happiest moments, the moments I treasure, are our everyday, ordinary moments together. A life full of those moments...perfect.

I flip the page, and it's blank. My cheeks are soaked. His hand falls to mine.

"Maggie, I know you've already moved on. But I hated how we left things. I had a lot I had to work through. I didn't treat you well. But it wasn't because I didn't love you. If anything, I love you too much. I've always loved you, and I always will." He sniffs and gazes down at his lap. "We'll always have our friendship. If you ever decide you want more, then I want you to know..."

His cheeks are red, all the way to his ears.

"Know what?"

He shoves the notebook forward a bit. "I didn't write it down. I didn't have this part planned out. And it doesn't matter, anyway. You've moved on. But I need you to know. You're everything to me. And I wish I'd been stronger, sooner."

I push him back on the sofa and kiss him. When my lips first touch his, there's no movement. He pulls back, searching my face. He squints, questioning. I nod.

"Really?"

I nod again, and he dips his head, his arms circle around my back, and we're both crying as we kiss.

"What about Xander?" His cheeks are flushed, his breathing heavy.

"That was a first date. I'll cancel it."

He pulls my head down so our lips collide while he holds me close, cupping my ass. Our tongues tangle as my emotions spiral. His sinewy form is both familiar and new. He tugs on my shirt, and I stop.

"Wait. Not on the sofa. Bedroom."

With an all-knowing grin, he asks, "Why?"

I don't bother answering him but tug him down the hall to my bedroom. When he sees my bed, he pauses. "Wait."

I freeze.

"I might not be able to give you children."

I gasp, letting the air I'd been withholding go, and half-laugh, "What?"

"My fertility. It might have been impacted. I've never been tested. I didn't ask many questions when I was going through chemo. We had sex without protection, and you didn't get pregnant."

I place my hands possessively on his hips. "I don't care."

"But children are important to you."

"Jason." He scowls as we eye each other. "I'm almost thirty-three. It could be me. I wouldn't be the first woman who had trouble conceiving. Would you not want to be with me if my fertility is the issue?"

"I wouldn't care. All I want is you. But you want children."

I want to shake him. "Jason, I want you. I want a future with you. Whatever that looks like. Good days. Bad days. I want them all. I want *all* the ordinary moments."

He presses his lips to mine. On an exhale, he whispers, "Me too." With his forehead pressed to mine, he asks, "Well, think we should start trying?"

"Huh?"

"We both want children. Why not? We can fly to Vegas next weekend and get married. If we're going to have trouble conceiving, the earlier we get working on it, the better, right?"

"You know, not everyone gets pregnant the moment they have sex, right? Just because we didn't initially doesn't mean it couldn't happen." I glance over my shoulder at the bed. "Today, even."

He lifts me up and tosses me. My body bounces ever so slightly on top of my flowery comforter. "If it happens, I'd be happy."

"Happy?"

"Ecstatic. Thrilled. Over the fucking moon. How's that?"

"This is crazy, you know that?"

He crawls up onto the bed, kicking off his running shoes. He caresses my face as his eyes glisten. My breath catches as I take him in. His lips fall to mine, and any worry falls away. Our kiss is tender and slow. He takes his time, removing my shirt, then my jeans and panties, then my bra, tracing soft, sweet kisses all along my bare, sensitized skin.

It's heaven, but the summer light shines brightly, and I grow self-conscious beneath his gaze. I cover my small breasts with one arm, and he stops me and kisses each finger while shaking his head.

"Don't hide from me." He kisses my lips. "Maggie." Drops a kiss on my chin. "You." A kiss on my neck. "Are." The kiss below my ear scatters goosebumps everywhere. "Perfect."

His mouth closes over one of my nipples. The sensation is exquisite. "I dream of you." His teeth clamp down, teasing, and I squeal. "Have for years." He places a light kiss over my heart. "Only you." Another kiss. "It's always been you."

He trails kisses down, and I know where he's going, but I stop him and pull him up to me. We have the rest of our lives for foreplay. "I want you."

He pulls back and studies me as I yank on his shirt to pull it over his head.

"We've waited long enough."

He licks his lips and smiles. Kisses me. "I couldn't agree more."

Together, we remove his remaining clothes, laughing when his jeans jam around one ankle.

I crawl back up the bed and lie beside him. He rests his body over mine, and I open my legs around him. Resting on one elbow, he fingers my hair and caresses my cheek.

"I love you, Maggie. For always. It was always you. And it always will be."

As we kiss, it hits me. Our love is soft, slow, and permanent.

He pulls back and touches my cheek.

"Tears?"

"Happy. The happiest of tears."

When he enters me, I shudder. We move as one. I am his, and he is mine. He makes love to me like no one ever has. Soft, slow, and tender, with raw emotion. Eyes open, studying my every reaction to his every thrust, his every movement that claims me in every way. We lift each other up to a blissful, soul-shattering release.

We cling to each other after as our breathing calms. I play with his short strands and place kisses all along his jawline until I hit damp skin.

"You're crying?" I ask.

"Happy tears."

"I love you so much."

"You'll never know, Maggie." He bends his head as I run the pad of my thumb over his eyebrow, his gaze laser-focused on me. "There's no way you can possibly ever know how much I love you. But know this, I will always love you more."

"You can't measure love. You can't compare love. You just have to accept it. Treasure it. Never let it go."

He drops a kiss on the tip of my nose and sighs.

"I should have come here with a ring, ready to propose. I should've...I guess I didn't let myself hope."

"What did you think would happen?"

We're both lying naked on top of my comforter, and he reaches to the bottom of the bed for the throw and pulls it over both of us, then falls back onto the pillows, settling me against him. Once we're settled, he answers me.

"I didn't know what would happen. I knew I couldn't leave things the way they were. Shannon, my therapist, told me—well, suggested—I tell you everything. Everything about how I feel. Everything I want for you. But I didn't know. I didn't have the courage to ask you if you'd started dating someone. When I saw Xander, I assumed I was too late."

"Oh, shit. Xander. I need to cancel tonight."

"Yes. You do."

"What should I tell him?"

"That we're getting married, and he can fuck off."

"Jason..."

"Too harsh?"

"Yeah. He's a good guy."

He traces kisses all along my throat and back up to my lips. "Maybe. But you're mine."

"Are you really considering moving here?"

He pulls back and sighs as he gazes at my breasts. They're

really nothing to look at. I raise up on my elbow, onto my side, to face him. He trails kisses from my nipple all along my chest, my neck, and up to my lips.

"I don't think you understand. I'm definitely moving here. I love you. I'm in love with you and have been since we were nineteen. It took me a long time to get here, to the point where I could let myself believe I could give you enough. But if you want a life with me, I want it to start immediately."

"But wouldn't the University of Chicago be a step down from Columbia?"

He returns his attention to my breasts, then cups my ass and pulls me next to his body and rolls onto his side, so we're facing each other. "Maybe. But I'm working on something else. I've been talking to Sam and Jackson about becoming an analyst for their VC group. I can do it from anywhere, and I'm ready for something other than academia. I wasn't exactly rocking the academic world. It turns out students didn't find my lectures to be overly stimulating, and I rather hated attempting to get work published."

"Then why the interview?"

"I might teach a class or two. Maybe. It also gave me an excuse for coming here. An excuse to see you."

I reach up and run my fingers through his hair, down to his jaw, over his short beard. He positions himself between my legs, bracing himself above me on bent arms, bending to trail kisses across my collarbone.

"You know, it's kind of hard to believe we made love and you're still here. You didn't run for the door or freak out." He collapses on the bed beside me with a grunt.

"I didn't freak out." His denial is instantaneous. Is he lying to himself or to me?

I lift myself up on my elbow, putting distance between us. He pulls me back down onto his chest.

"Okay. Yes, I did. But only because I want the most for you. And now? I still do. I still think you can do better than me. But I know it's not possible for you to find someone who loves you more than I do. If, for whatever crazy reason, you want me, and you want a life with me, then I'll try my best to give you everything."

"So, we're officially stepping outside of the friend zone?"

"Officially." He pushes me onto my back and hovers over me, his lips inches from mine. "I think we crossed the friend zone line a long time ago, if we're honest."

He questions me, the skin around the corners of his eyes wrinkling, silently asking if I agree. I do. I silently affirm and close the distance between us.

When he kisses me, like always, I lose track of rational thought. The sensation is surreal, dreamlike. Almost unbelievable. But when his scruffy beard chafes my bare skin and his dark eyes penetrate mine, full of promise, then I'm reassured it's not a dream. We've crossed the line. This, right here, is my happy.

epilogue - jason

Jason

"There's still time to run, man." Chase claps a hand on my shoulder with a broad smile.

"Are you kidding? This guy's been pining over this girl almost as long as I can remember. I'm surprised he hasn't taken her to the justice of the peace already just to get it done." Sam kicks his legs up on his outdoor coffee table, beer in hand.

Sam knows me well. I've offered many times to go to Vegas, to make it official, and let the shindig in her parents' back yard be a celebration with friends. I've offered to marry her in front of our friends, every single year if she wants. But no, Maggie's a traditionalist, and she's had visions of her wedding for years. I want her dreams to come true. For Maggie, that's a wedding in her parents' back yard among family and friends, and if that's what she wants, that's what we'll do.

I'm living with her now, for all intents and purposes. We flew back to clean out my empty apartment since it sold. I signed the papers this afternoon. We're staying here at Sam's place this weekend, in his guest room, which is substantially nicer than my old apartment. Sam wanted to give me a traditional bachelor party, just like Yara and Zoe desperately wanted to do a traditional bachelorette, but Maggie and I aren't so into the big drunken parties. We finally arrived at a night out with friends, a sort of combination bachelor and bachelorette.

We get married in two weeks, and I can't wait. You wouldn't think it would matter that much to me. I never spent much time thinking about marriage, mainly because I didn't see it as a possibility for me. But once I decided to do it, to let go and go for it, everything changed. I'm counting down the days until Maggie becomes my wife.

I choose to ignore Chase. He's a friend of these guys, but I don't feel the need to respond to his ridiculous comments. He's always cracking jokes, to the point it's hard to know if he's a decent guy. Anna and Jackson vouch for him, though, and they all go way back.

The whole collective crew is meeting up at Sam and Olivia's place before going out. Sam has the evening planned, and I don't doubt we're in for an unforgettable night.

"Yeah, I never thought I'd see this guy smile so much. Remember how worried we used to get about him?" Ollie asks, directing his question to Sam.

"Remember? It's been an ongoing topic with Mom for years. Hell, we broke into his apartment last year," Sam says.

Maggie's inside, talking with friends, her hair blown out, shiny and smooth. She's wearing high, strappy heels and a short dress that shows off her long, lean legs. I watch her lift her glass and swirl her drink while talking, animated.

"Well, he may be happy, but the dude still doesn't talk much," Chase says, feet propped up on the fire pit coffee table.

"Hey, I'm sitting right here." They all chuckle like it's so funny. I'm fully aware I don't talk much. If I have something to say, I say it.

Chase brought a woman with him tonight. Since I've known him, he's been more of a "meeting up later for drinks" kind of guy. Since the ladies are in the kitchen, visible but inaudible behind the glass doors, I decide to turn the tables and tease the joker.

"What about you? Any plans in the works with Sydney?" I ask, shifting the conversation away from me.

His mouth gapes open as he points toward the kitchen. "That woman? No way. Absolutely not."

"What? Why did you bring her?" It's not like he needed a date. He never has a date. He prefers late-night booty calls.

"She's new at work. Doesn't know anyone here. She was hanging out in my office, said she didn't have any plans tonight. I brought her to be nice. But no, it's not like that between us. She's not my type at all. Serious work bitch, like to the nth degree. Every conversation circles back to work. And need I remind you we work at an accounting firm."

I glance over at Sydney. She's wearing an attractive pantsuit with serious heels. I do agree they aren't each other's type. She's far more sophisticated than Chase. He's in a t-shirt under a blazer with jeans. Today's t-shirt reads *Screw your lab safety, I want superpowers*.

Maggie's engaged in a conversation with Sydney, apart from the other women. That's my Maggie. She'll make any person feel welcome and at home. All the girls went out today for a New York spa and shopping day, got nails, hair, and makeup done, all courtesy of Olivia and Sam. Maggie isn't doing professional hair and makeup for our wedding, since we'll be in Iowa at her parents' place, so Anna and Olivia wanted to give her a special day here. Since Sydney was the one girl who didn't partake, I don't doubt Maggie feels the need to give her extra attention and include her now.

My foot gets kicked off the coffee table, and the movement shocks me.

"Think you can stop looking at her for a bit and join in the conversation?" Ollie asks with his signature shit-eating grin.

"I don't want to stop. Ever." I stare him down. I don't care what these guys think.

"Hey, Sam. Double or nothing. Remember? Hand it over." Ollie holds his hand out to Sam.

"No, no, no. I'm the one who said they'd be married within two years. You hand it over."

"No, my original bet, from the one made like ten years ago, was no time cap. And you bet five years, then you said two when you lost that one. I believe you owe me."

"Shut it. You owe me two Ben Franklins," Sam says before tossing back his beer.

Ollie laughs but makes no move to pay his brother back.

Chase holds his beer out then points it at Jason.

"Hold on. Ten years, you've been friends? That's twisted. The only woman I've been friends with for that long is Anna, and I couldn't imagine—"

"You didn't have *that kind* of friendship with Anna." Jackson's voice booms across the room. He had been standing farther out on the terrace on his cell. Guess he finished his call. He seems more exasperated by Chase than offended.

Chase holds up his hands. "Dude. I didn't mean it like that. I'm just saying, if I'm friends with someone for that long, I can't imagine it turning into more. That's all I'm saying."

"Well, in our case, it was complicated. I always wanted more. You wait until you meet the one," I say looking over to her again through the glass.

"Well, not me, lads. Some of us like being single." Chase raps against his chest. Sam and Ollie smirk in an almost identical way, and Jackson shakes his head. Once again, I find myself wanting to ignore these guys, so I shift to watch Maggie. She tilts her head back, laughing at something someone inside said.

"Damn, bro, you can't stop looking at her. Was it always this way, and I just didn't notice?" Ollie asks.

"Yeah, it's always been this way," Sam answers, looking at his brother like he's dense.

"I don't understand what took you ten years. She's looked at you with goo-goo eyes since the day we met her. Mom spent years asking me if anything was going on with you two," Ollie pipes back.

"You know what, I'm not getting into that with you guys. It took me a while, okay? She was my best friend, and I didn't want to risk losing her. You guys think it's all easy. It's not always easy. Plus, we met in college. Do you guys even still talk to the women you dated in college?" My question shuts them up. When you meet your other half in college, it's not always a smooth path forward, because when you're young, you're kind of half-baked. And I had some difficult things I needed to accept. Not that I'm going to go into any of that with these guys.

Ollie takes a long swallow from his beer, the glass hiding the grin I know is plastered on his face, because he loves to tease the shit out of me, and Chase sits up, setting an empty beer on the table. He reaches out and pats my knee.

"Glad it eventually worked out, man. I'm gonna run in and get another beer. Anyone else need one?"

Sam checks his watch. "Help yourself, but we'll be leaving soon. Probably in less than fifteen minutes."

Sam's pronouncement has Ollie and Jackson heading inside, following Chase.

As they step through the automatic sliding door, Maggie slips by them. She falls onto my lap, and I breathe her in. There's a strong, pungent scent that's not her at all, and I assume it's the hairspray. I don't mind. When I lift her hair and kiss below her ear, she wiggles on my lap, and I groan. What I wouldn't give for us to be back at our apartment, just the two of us.

"You ready for tonight?" she asks.

"With you by my side, I can handle anything."

epilogue - maggie

Maggie

"Everything's set. Will has lit the candles in the hall, and guests are starting to arrive. Are you ready?" Zoe brims with exhilaration. She's excited for me, the same way I was for her four years ago at her wedding. Her hand falls to my shoulder, and she spins me to face the full-length mirror in our parents' bedroom.

She and I grew up in this house. Almost all my childhood memories center around this home or this neighborhood. We have photos of Zoe and me, both toddlers, playing in the clean laundry in this room, in front of this mirror.

Zoe rests her chin on my exposed shoulder. "You look beautiful."

I'm wearing a simple 1930s inspired white gown. The silk chiffon is embroidered and beaded and features kimono-style cap sleeves and an asymmetrical wrap-style bodice. It's a gown I found on Etsy from Martin McCrea Couture. After the wedding, I plan to shorten the hemline so I can wear it again in the future. My hair is down, but the sides are pulled back, and daisies have been woven in through the braids in the back.

There's a soft knock on the door before Mom enters. She gasps and immediately fans her face. "I can't cry. I'm gonna ruin my makeup. Oh, my word, you two are so beautiful. How has time passed so quickly? It feels like yesterday I was dumping you both in the bathtub when you played with paints or mud."

Her voice cracks as Zoe and I hug her. Tears come to my eyes, and I break away because I don't want my mascara to run. I step to the window looking out over the back yard.

There's a wedding arch placed at the end of the aisle, wrapped in sheer white fabric, with a green and white flower arrangement looped through the curve of the arch. Rows and rows of the white rental chairs are lined up, with perfectly mowed green grass flooring the aisle. Buckets of sea spray daisies adorn the end of each aisle.

The centerpieces on the tables for the reception mimic the sea spray daisies in glass mason jars, wrapped with tiny golden lights, reminiscent of the fireflies Zoe and I used to catch as kids. Zoe, Yara, and I sat around last night after the rehearsal dinner creating them. The afternoon sun shines brightly. It's a perfect summer day, even if it is a touch warmer than we'd prefer. As the sun sets and the evening reception begins, it will be perfect.

People are filling the rows. I search for Jason, but I don't see him. He's probably inside, waiting for instructions. I still pinch myself, unable to believe we're actually doing this. That we made it. In some ways, it feels like we're already an old couple. We know everything about each other. In other ways, it all feels new.

My face warms as I think about all the places we've christened in our new apartment. I'm still not pregnant, after two months of unprotected sex. I'm not going to worry about it, though. We've agreed that if after another month I'm still not pregnant, I'll meet with my doctor, but from what I've read, she won't tell me to do anything until it's been six months. I'm not worried. Whatever happens will happen. Jason and I will face it together. There are no certainties in life. I'm kind of glad we're walking down the aisle, facing the unknown together. If we were already pregnant, there would be more certainty to our future, and I feel like we need to be brave together. This is significant for us. We have concerns and worries, but they don't matter. What matters is we will lean on each other to get through whatever comes our way.

The door opens again, and Yara enters. Zoe is my maid of honor, and Yara is my bridesmaid. Sam is Jason's best man, and Ollie is his groomsman. We could have easily had bigger bridal parties, but I hate asking others to partake in the expense of purchasing the outfits, and I want simple. We have a slew of honorary bridesmaids and groomsmen, all honored in our ceremony programs.

Yara stands in the doorway. "It's time."

My bridesmaids are both in similar soft yellow, or buttercream, sundresses. Yara is wearing platform sandals with a punk vibe, and Zoe is wearing white sandals that are one step above flip flops. They're both so different, and I love how even in similar dresses their personalities shine through.

As I make my way down the stairs, flashes of my childhood fall before me. Sliding down the stairs back when my parents had carpet on them, getting yelled at for attempting to slide down the banister, parading down these stairs in my prom dress. This is why I wanted to get married at my childhood home. I love all my memories.

We journey through the house, and then step out onto the back porch. All heads turn our way, and everyone stands. One of my childhood friends, a neighbor from down the street, strums the chords to *Somewhere Over the Rainbow* by Israel Kamakawiwo'ole. It's not a traditional wedding song, but it's a song that has spoken to me for as long as I can remember.

Zoe smiles, takes my niece's hand, and walks down the aisle. Yara falls in behind them.

When it's my turn, I stand on the grass, my heels sinking slightly into the soft soil. My father stands to my side, tears glimmering. "You ready, sweetie pie?"

"More than ready."

My arm falls on my father's, and we step with a practiced rhythm. I smile at friends and family as we pass, but my focus centers on Jason. He's not crimson, but there's a noticeable ruddy hue to his complexion. It's a warm day, and he's in a tux, so that could be it, but I'd be willing to bet he's nervous. Those eyes I know so well lock on mine, and everything else fades to black.

Dad bends and kisses my forehead and joins my mother in the front row.

Jason takes my hands in his. My heart vibrates, and the world slips away. It's just the two of us. Sam's father, Mr. Duke, is acting as our officiant. He speaks of love, and what it means, and directs us to say our vows.

We both wrote our own vows. Jason lifts my hand to his

lips. Tears simmer, on the verge of spilling over, but these are tears of joy.

"Maggie, when I researched wedding vows, I found the traditional ones, the vows promising through sickness and in health, 'til death do us part. I've been so afraid, not of death, but of hurting you, and those vows simply don't say enough. I promise to love you and cherish you, for all the rest of our days. You are the most important person in my life. My best friend. The love of my life. My partner in life. If I could, I would give you not only this life but all my future lives. Since I can't give what probably doesn't exist, I give you all my tomorrows, and I promise to do my best to stay rooted in the present. No matter what we might face, I am yours, today, tomorrow, always."

Tears stream down my face, and I pause to swipe at them. He leans to kiss me, and Mr. Duke intervenes with a deep, "Not yet, son." Laughter echoes through our family and friends.

"Jason, you have been my best friend, confidante, and my greatest challenge." I pause as more laughter rings through, even from Jason.

"You make me happier than I ever thought possible. My most favorite memories are with you, and I am so grateful to spend the rest of my life creating more cherished moments. Let us build a home of laughter, love, and support. Let us create a warm and loving space for the good times and the bad. Let us be a home for each other, forever and ever." I pause, searching for his words. "Jason, no matter what we might face together, I am yours, today, tomorrow, always."

Mr. Duke steps forward and asks Jason to repeat after him. We both get our turn to say, "I do," and when he drawls out, "Noooowwww, you can kiss the bride," everyone laughs.

Later on, when it's time for our first dance, Jason leads me onto the dance floor we created. We strung Christmas lights all through the trees, and the twinkling lights create a natural shimmering canopy. *The Luckiest* from Ben Folds begins. He chose it, and it's perfect for us. We got lost along the way, or maybe sidetracked. I suppose our path to where we are now has been longer than most, but without a doubt, we are the luckiest.

THE END

Curious about the McLoughlin Charity? All questions are answered in *Chasing Frost*.

Read Chase's story, Chasing Frost, next...

Her slender fingers slip into mine and hot damn. I'm not even sure where to look first. She's all-natural, with glossy pale pink lips and a rosy blush to her cheeks.

"Sydney Frost." Her hand leaves mine and she places those dark eyes on the others in our group. Frosty. I like it.

"Sydney will be joining our firm" It's official. I'm in lust.

Turns out there's just one problem. She's an undercover FBI agent, and I'm her main suspect.

notes, background, and message to readers

A long, long time ago, I read *P.S. I Love You* by Barbara Conklin. I cried and cried and cried. I think I might have been fifteen, and the story ripped me apart. Little footnote, I haven't read it since then, so who knows if it would hit me the same way now, or if my memory of it is even correct. I found it used for $42 and decided that was too much to spend.

Anyway...in the book, her first love dies. I can't remember if they are in high school or college. But I feel like he might have been from California. For years and years, I've wondered what happened to her. Did she fall in love again?

That's kind of the genesis for this book. When I was coming up with Sam's story, for some reason, I decided he needed a friend who was down and struggling. A friendship that showed his true colors. Then I had to decide why his friend seemed so down, and there you have it. He became the friend of Maggie's first love.

As I did the research for this book, I found some real

tear-jerker memoirs, as you can imagine. The one I had to take breaks from in order to finish reading it is *Somebody Up There Hates Me* by Hollis Seamon. The fictional book is based on her observations of teenagers in a hospice ward when her son was a patient. I highly recommend this book. It's a tear-jerker, but it's also so insightful into how we all cope with death.

Everything Happens for a Reason by Kate Bowler is another book I came across that, well, bowled me over. Bowler currently battles cancer (and from what I hear, from a friend of a friend, she's doing well), but her perspective and her experience with the prosperity gospel is not only insightful, you'll find yourself laughing.

I also read many blogs and found one common thread. At a certain point, many people who blogged about their struggles with cancer reached a point they didn't want to talk about it anymore. Every now and then, I found some who did mention some of the long-term struggles they individually faced. Not every person who has cancer will continue to struggle with it, but some will.

It's one thing to fear cancer, earthquakes, war, and asteroids from a theoretical perspective. It's another to come face to face with any of these things and then move forward. There's no way every person's individual experience will be the same as all others. But this is how I envisioned one person *might* experience it.

When writing this book, my beta readers helped me tremendously. I owe a debt of gratitude to Robbie Carnaggio, Jenny Pezzano, Keri James, Anna, and Ashley Hasty of Hasty's Booklist for taking so much time and care to read through and provide valuable feedback.

To achieve my goal of providing a quality Indie novel, I

work with several editors, and I'd like to thank each of them. Development editor AmyClaire Major, Editor Lori Whitwam, and Line Editor Heather Whitehead of Capstone Dalmatians.

Thanks so much for reading.

also by isabel jolie

Arrow Tactical Security Series

Better to See You (Wolf and Alexandria)

Sure of One (Jack and Ava)

Cloak of Red (Sophia and Fisher)

Stolen Beauty (Knox and Sage)

Savage Beauty (Max and Sloane) - Releasing June 6th

Sinful Beauty (Tristan and Lucia) - Releasing September 12th

Gilded Saint (Sam and Willow) - Releasing December 5th

The Twisted Vines Series

Crushed (Erik and Vivi)

Breathe (Kairi and David)

Savor (Trevor and Stella)

Haven Island Series

Rogue Wave (Tate and Luna)

Adrift (Gabe and Poppy)

First Light (Logan and Cali)

The West Side Series

Blurred Lines (Jackson and Anna)

Trust Me (Sam Duke and Olivia)

Finding Delilah (Delilah and Mason)

Forgetting Him (Jason and Maggie)

Chasing Frost (Chase and Sadie)

Misplaced Mistletoe (Ashton aka Dr. Bobby and Nora)

Standalone Romances

How to Survive a Holiday Fling (Oliver Duke and Kate)

Always Sunny (Ian Duke and Sandra)

The Romantics (Harrison and Zuri)

about the author

Isabel Jolie, aka Izzy, lives on a lake, loves dogs of all stripes, and if she's not working, she can be found reading, often with a glass of wine. In prior lives, Izzy worked in marketing and advertising, in a variety of industries, such as financial services, entertainment, and technology. In this life, she loves daydreaming and writing contemporary romances with real, flawed characters with inner strength.

Sign-up for Izzy's newsletter to keep up-to-date on new releases, promotions and giveaways. (**Pro-tip** - She offers a free book on her home page…just scroll down after arriving at her site.)

Buy ebooks and signed paperbacks direct from Isabel at www.isabeljoliebooks.com

Want to say hi? Email her through her website or reply to her newsletter…she loves to hear from readers.